D. ANDERSON

Suplexed Into Love

Model: Isaac Dawson

Photographer: Dave DeCaro (davelandweb.com)

Cover Designed by Jenny Steve-James

First edition

ISBN: 979-8-9875430-0-9

This book was professionally typeset on Reedsy.
Find out more at reedsy.com

Contents

Chapter One:

I sit at my desk with the phone receiver pressed to my ear, with upbeat light music still playing. I am still on hold for what seems like ages. The music may seem calming, but it was not calming the agitation I have. I am beyond annoyed that I even have to make this call, it was the third time today that I had to call the IT department. I am tapping my pen against my desk while staring blankly at the black screen of doom on my computer. Being on the phone with the IT department is not a part of my job description but as the boss around here, someone has to do it.

I look at the two employees that are in my office today, Stephanie and Crystal. Stephanie has been my best friend since Elementary school and Crystal is a new hire that had seemed to become like our third amigo. Upper management often put us three together to work at these headquarters. We are the home base for all the EMTs, paramedics, lifeguards, first aid and all things in terms of medical attention. We know who is on shift at any given time to get to any medical emergency in the hotel.

We all have to carry these ridiculous walkie talkies; the medical response is designated to certain radio channels. Stephanie is holding the designated office one while the mobile ones we take out on the floor are docked. I slam the receiver down after I can't handle the hold music anymore. Without our computers working, I can't work on any of the stacked-up reports that I am behind on inputting.

"Well, you guys are free to go until tomorrow." I sigh out, I lean back in my office chair defeated.

"Ok, boss lady." Stephanie says as she moves to stand up, "What's your damage?"

"Stuck here until at least 2200." I said shaking the computer mouse hoping that it'll magically work now but still nothing.

"Are they that backed up?" Crystal asks as she pulls her work jacket on.

"Between the front desk computers going down and the big wrestling pay-per-view tonight, IT is tapped out. Nothing has changed since the last time I called." I huff out.

"Who's working the event?" Stephanie asks curiously. She walks up to the schedules that are pinned up on the cork board.

"I will be here now, thanks to the IT department." I said, turning to look at her.

"I'm going to make a round on the casino floor before I clock out. Stephanie, you want to come?" Crystal asked, picking up her designated walkie talkie and clipping it to the ugly yellow EMT cargo pants.

"I'll catch up, I have to talk to Tara about something." Stephanie said. Crystal nods before she heads out of the office. Stephanie needing to talk to me privately was never good. My stomach drops in panic, what was so important that she had to talk with me privately?

"What's up?" I ask twirling in my chair to look at the long brunette-haired fair skinned friend of mine that just now sat on the edge of my desk.

"When was the last time you went on a date?"

"That's a bit personal."

"Come on Tara, I'm your best friend. We can be open about these kinds of things. I have sat back and watched you work eighteen-to-twenty-two-hour shifts. I was there for all the life struggles you have been through. From your dad leaving, your mom being a struggling single mom, and I even came to the hospital when your sister died." Stephanie says. With the mention of my sister's death, my head turns slightly to be able to view the framed photo of mom, Xavier, and me. "You haven't dated since Dave left you over Xavier, have you?"

"No, but Dave was right. What man would want to date a single mom? You know how hard it is to find a guy who will be okay with becoming a stepdad."

"Meg asked you to adopt Xavier, she didn't want you to put your life on hold. Meg would want you to still live your life and to find true love." Stephanie said as I glanced back at her.

"The point, Stephanie?"

"There's this cruise…"

"Absolutely not. You know that I can't afford that."

"Hear me out. Your mom has already agreed to watch Xavier and I pitched in for the first payment."

"You talked with my mom and already booked my room with partial payment?" I asked shocked and angered at the same time. I felt trapped into going on this cruise, I didn't have a choice to decide for myself. A part of me wanted to be excited to go because for six years I've been a hard-working single mom. I've worked every day to make ends meet and long hours to make everything worth it.

I wanted Xavier to have the best life that I knew Meg would have given him and how she would want me to raise him. Guilt began to chew at me that maybe Stephanie was right. I haven't been living nor have I let Xavier live the life my sister would want him to have due to working as much as I have.

"Yes, you need this time girl. It's a singles cruise so every person there is ready to mingle, and you may even hook up with someone. Lord knows you probably haven't gotten any action in just as long—there's probably cobwebs up there by now."

I tossed my pen at her with a chuckle, "Shut up!" A few more chuckles escape, and I was looking down at my lap in disbelief that she just said that. She's taking me on a singles cruise to meet someone. Did she really say a singles cruise? "Singles cruise?"

"Yep, a cruise filled with eligible men and women."

"Do I have to go?"

"Yes, just enjoy yourself. Even if you don't meet anyone, I want you to have fun." Stephanie said in hopes that I'll go for it. I wanted to go because if anything I did need a break. "Anyways, the next payment is in two weeks and the cruise is in six weeks. A payment every two weeks and pay the remainder when you check in. I'll text you all the information, I'm sure Crystal is wondering where I'm at." Stephanie said, standing up from my desk to go find Crystal out on the casino floor.

"Stephanie?" I asked. She stopped in the doorway, turned to look at me to hear what I had to say, "Thanks for always looking out for me."

Chapter One:

"That's what best friends are for." She said with a bright smile.

"But I still hate you for planning this and getting my mom involved. You're dead." I chuckled. She rolled her eyes before she pulled the door shut behind her. I turned in my chair to get a better view of the framed photo of my small family. I leaned forward to pull the picture into my lap. I haven't lived fully since Xavier was born. I live and breathe being a mom and dedicated worker, that's all I know.

Meg was my older sister who had gone down so many wrong paths, but she was my big sister. She got pregnant from some deadbeat who constantly abused her every which way possible. She ran when she found out she was pregnant with his kid. Meg made me promise that the father would *NEVER* see or set a finger on the child. I also had to promise that if anything happened to her, I'd take sole custody of her child.

Come delivery, my mom and I drove her to the hospital in excitement for the baby to be born. During delivery, Meg hemorrhaged and couldn't be saved. I named him what Meg wanted him to be named, Xavier James. I had filed a lot of paperwork, went to numerous court hearings, gone to various interviews and even had my house inspected before Xavier was allowed to come home with me. I would never regret the decision in adopting Xavier, I wouldn't want it any other way nor would I want him to fall into the system.

At that time, I was engaged to Dave. I thought he was the one. I loved him so much. When I went through the adoption process, it had caused so many fights between us. Dave didn't understand why I would want to adopt Xavier. I think he just wasn't ready to be a dad or didn't want to be a dad period. When he called off the wedding, I was devastated. It had left

5

me so broken hearted that I had closed myself off from love. What man would be willing to be a dad? Dave certainly didn't. I didn't want to go through the heartbreak again, my heart was still so fragile.

I push the frame back to where it belongs on my desk. I lean back in my chair with my hands holding my head up. I'm thankful that I took custody of Xavier, but Stephanie is right. I gave up living my own life because I'm a single mom. *I need to take a walk.* I think. I stand up and grab my walkie talkie to take with me.

I approach the door, flicking the lights off before pulling the door open. I didn't realize that there was anyone trying to come in and almost collide into a man on crutches. The man is about my height with shaggy dirty blonde hair.

"Whoa…" he said, stumbling a little. I grab him before he can fully fall over.

"Sorry, I didn't know anyone was coming in." I said helping get him resituated on his crutches.

"No problem. I was informed this was the place to go for a wheelchair rental?"

"We do have wheelchairs, but they aren't rentals. Wait, aren't you the guy who broke his leg last week at the training facility?" I ask propping the door open so I will be able to continue talking with him. I walk back into the office retrieving a wheelchair for him.

"That's me, I'm Chris." He answered. I roll a chair around the door, lock the wheelchair in place so it won't move when he tries to sit down. Chris maneuvers himself to where he is positioned the right way to sit in the wheelchair.

"Your doctor put a cast on you, what did they determine?"

"Torn ACL and torn meniscus. Bum knee. Surgery to repair

it and out of the ring for six weeks minimum." He explained.

"Well Chris, you'll be my special project then. You going to the pay-per-view tonight?"

"Yep, are you wheeling me down there?"

"I have nothing else to do. I have to wait for IT to come fix the computers, but they are swamped until ten." I begin to push him around the casino floor. The slot machines chiming as we walked by and hearing screams of victory when people won. We get to the ramp that will take us to the underbelly of the hotel, it is an employee only area.

The hotel owner worked closely with the local wrestling promotion to build the hotel's very own, state of the art training facility. The facility is used by all the wrestlers for training, seminars, their weekly television taping, and these pay-per-views. Personally, I don't follow wrestling, so I don't know the first thing on how it was decided. I just knew that my department has gotten a lot of calls from injuries. "Are you watching the PPV? Or sitting in the back?"

"I'm going to be watching tonight, I'm still obligated to come. You are going to see a lot of me because I have to continue to lift weights and stay in somewhat good physical shape."

"You have a long recovery though; those are some major injuries you sustained last week. How did you even get that hurt?"

"I don't even remember but I hope that I never have to experience that pain again."

"I hope so too. Do you want me to take you out to the handicap seating?"

"Actually, could you take me backstage? I have to clock in and make my way around to see the guys." Chris said as I pushed the down button for the elevator. We wait for the elevator to arrive, so we can go down two floors to the entrance to the locker rooms. The ride on the elevator was so quiet that I could hear the soft music playing over the sound system. I wheel him off towards the locker room.

"Do you have anyone to escort you out to the arena?"

"I got it from here. How do I get the wheelchair back to you?" He asked, twirling his chair around by himself. He must have used a wheelchair before if he was able to maneuver himself so easily.

"I could give you my cell number or I'll just show up when this thing usually ends to escort you back."

"How late are you working?"

"Now that you're here, I'm guessing later than I was originally scheduled. I still have IT coming by to try to get our computers up and running again."

"Well, you are booked. Thank you, um—"

"Tara." I answered. I push the handicap button to get the double doors to start opening, the springs on the doors were so rusted that it takes longer to open. "You got it from here?"

"I hope so, this isn't my first rodeo using a wheelchair. This chair will be my best friend indefinitely. Your phone number?"

"Right, your phone?" I asked. He shifts in the chair pulling his phone out from a butt pocket. Chris hands me the phone, I enter my number and push the call button to hear my phone ringing. I give Chris his phone back and push the handicap button again to keep the doors open longer.

"Thanks. I will see you in a few." He spoke. Chris spun himself around, I stand there watching him roll through the double doors and down the hallway filled with crew members and wrestlers prepping for tonight's show. I make sure he had made it through the double doors before I turn on my heels to head back to my office.

I sit in my chair listening to the walkie talkie for all first responders to see if any apply to me. I leave the lights off and close my eyes to try to catch up on some shut eye since I had been here since 0300.

I feel my phone vibrating in my pocket, my eyes were so heavy that it is hard to come out of my relaxed state. I rub at my eyes hoping it'll wake me up enough to check my phone.

"'Last match is about to begin; you might want to head down.'" Chris texted. I look at the time, it is now 2230 and IT still hasn't shown up. I stand up clipping the walkie talkie to my fire hydrant-colored pants before walking out of the office to go help Chris.

I make my way out to the arena's handicap seats. Chris sits on his lonesome, hunched over in his chair and head hung low. His arms are crossed in his lap. I sit down on the metal bench beside him.

"How was it?" I asked softly.

"Wish I could have participated." He said in a soft tone. He slumps further in his chair. "I'm out for months and expected to come every freaking day. It's like rubbing my face in it." I simply nod as he glances over to me, "You're not being paid enough to be a therapist."

"No, I'm not. I'm barely getting paid enough for how much they work me. The hotel has so much back pay they owe me that they are in debt to me." I joked, seeing a smile finally come to his face.

"I'll have them add my tab to their debt."

"Noted. I understand though Chris. I have dived so hard into my work that I lost a sense of myself. I haven't gone out to have fun in six years, much less on a date."

"That's pathetic." He said, as we both went quiet, "No offense."

"None taken. It's so bad that my best friend signed me up to go on some cruise in six weeks."

"Ok, you've made me feel better." He says as he is nothing but smiles. I stand up, unlocking his wheelchair and push him out of the arena. "A cruise in six weeks? I have to go on a cruise in six weeks too."

"Is that really smart given you have a bum knee?"

"Well, my work is paying for it. I have to attend it and there's no getting out of it."

"Lucky you. Just don't fall overboard then you'll never make it home."

"Real funny."

"How'd you get here, if you can't drive?"

"Uber." He answered. I push him through the casino to where the taxi lines are.

"Well, this is where we go our separate ways. You have my number, so don't be afraid to use it. Text me on your way tomorrow and I'll come greet you with your throne on wheels." I laugh out loud. Chris pulls himself to stand up and pushes the crutches under his pits.

"I'll see you tomorrow. By the time I'm healed, my butt will definitely be imprinted in that chair." He adds, getting us to laugh even more.

"I will name this chair after you then."

"I expect it to sparkle." He said with a bright smile. I've met a few wrestlers over my time employed here, Chris had to be the first one that had such a perfect smile.

"I'm going to make sure of it. Good night, Chris." I said turning the wheelchair around. I walk back into the casino, beeline back to my office to return the chair. I plop down in my office chair to rest some before the trek out to my car.

With a shake of my mouse to check the status of our computers, and to my surprise, my computer was working. I run a hand through my hair looking at the stack of reports that need to be inputted. I lean back in my office chair contemplating whether to stay or to go home. My eyesight lands on the hideous wheelchair I was just pushing Chris in.

Chris was really bummed from not being able to work the event tonight. I've never watched wrestling a day in my life but could imagine he was passionate about it. I tried to picture myself not being able to help my work team in a medical emergency.

I really should spruce that chair up for Chris, maybe it'll brighten his mood. I let out a sigh before I begin to rush through as many reports as I can before it strikes midnight.

I clock out and leave the rest of the reports to be dealt with tomorrow when I come in at 1300. I barely made it home without crashing my car from exhaustion. I climb out of my car, moving like a zombie through my house. I push my son's door open to peek in on him.

The Batman night light on his nightstand is on. It is illuminating the whole room. I quietly step in, standing at his bedside and resting my hand on his back. He is breathing and snoring away. I smile to myself.

"Good night, Xavier. I love you." I whispered. I walk back out of his room and leave the door cracked just a little. I walk into my room doing a belly flop onto my Cal King plush mattress. I am so tired from the twenty-one-hour shift that all I can think about is sleep.

"Mommy? Mommy?" Xavier's voice squeaked out. I am so

tired that I can't move an ounce, my eyes can't even open from exhaustion. "You aren't dead, are you?" Xavier asked with more concern. My eyes fling open after he said that, Xavier's blue eyes staring back at me. Xavier was just barely tall enough to peek over the height of my bed. I run a hand over my face trying to wake up more.

"No, just really tired. Why don't you turn on Batman and I'll order breakfast?" I asked as he nods. I watch Xavier walk out of the room in his black and gray Batman pajamas carrying the stuffed dinosaur he always slept with.

I reach for my phone ordering McDonald's to be delivered.

Xavier loves my pancakes but the pancake platter from McDonald's has to suffice for today. I make sure I order something for my mom before I check out.

My mom moved to state line, only a thirty-minute drive from here without traffic. On nights like last night, my mom will occupy the guest room.

I went into the connecting bathroom showering up and got into a new work outfit. I walked out right when the doorbell chimes that breakfast is here.

Chapter Two

I drive to the hotel after dropping Xavier off at kindergarten and doing a little shopping at Walmart. I park in the designated employee parking lot before walking to my office. I knew I was early for my shift, but it beats going home for thirty minutes. I let myself into the office seeing Stephanie and Crystal already working on the stack of reports that I couldn't get to last night.

"I thought you weren't in until 1300." Crystal said shocked when she saw me walk into the office.

"I'm not but I had to take Xavier to school and do a few things. Figured I'd head in instead of going home for a mere half hour." I explained. I drop the bags on my desk before sitting down in my office chair. I slide my lunch bag down by my feet for later. I begin to pull out all the craft stuff from the various gray and green plastic bags.

"What's that for?" Stephanie asks approaching my desk to put the reports in the complete basket.

"I'm making a savings jar for this cruise that you had gladly roped me into. And I have a wheelchair to spruce up."

"Why do you have to spruce up a wheelchair?"

"I want Chris to feel a little happier." I shrugged, not even looking up from the mason jar I was doodling on.

"Chris? Who is this Chris guy?" Stephanie asked with a perked brow. Coincidentally, Chris hobbles through the door at that exact moment. I look up when I hear the door click open.

"Afternoon Chris, you're early." I said putting the cap back on my sharpie. Stephanie looks over her shoulder at the six-foot blonde-haired blue-eyed man then back to me. Her expression softens a little, then smiles.

"He's cute." She whispered so he can't hear. I roll my eyes as he makes his way to my desk. He plops down in the free chair on the opposing side of my desk.

"I know. The boss wanted me to come in early to be inspected by the trainers or what not." He shrugged.

"Don't be too thrilled about it."

"Just as thrilled as you. Do you ever go home? You were just here."

"So were you." I retorted.

"Touché." He said when our walkie talkies begin to go crazy with a bunch of calls. We each grab one to listen to all the calls that are coming in. I look at the various printed schedules and try to make sense of all the medical emergencies that were happening.

"So, we have a DOA in room 15478, a drowning victim, and a cardiac arrest on the floor." I said, tapping my finger against my chin as I thought. "Crystal, go on the floor until we can get an additional ambulance on board." I instructed. Crystal nodded, slinging a medical bag onto her shoulder and clipped her receiver to her pants.

Crystal beelines out of the office. "Stephanie, why don't you go up and secure the room until the police and coroner arrive." I instructed as Stephanie grabbed her receiver to tend to that fiasco. Clicking the receiver in my hand, "Adam and Lisa, you read me?"

"Loud and clear." Adam's Barry White deep voice came over the stereo.

"Dang, his balls really dropped during puberty." Chris said, chuckling at himself. I let out a hefty laugh looking at him over my shoulder. I had to contain my laughter before I pushed the button to speak.

"Channel 7 Adam and Lisa. Home base out." I said clicking over to the other channel. "Home base calling for Adam and Lisa."

"Adam and Lisa hear you loud and clear."

"Drowning victim at the east side pool, conscious but shallow breathing. Patient has a slight gash on forehead. Need transport to St. Rose medical center. They have the shortest wait."

"On it. Over and out." Lisa said as I switch back to the main station we use. I look over the schedule. "Stephanie to one."

"Stephanie to base camp."

"Base camp hears you loud and clear. Is Alicia and Eve up there?"

"Yes, patient has not been moved from their original state. Alicia and Eve on standby to transport patient if the coroner doesn't show."

"I need them to transport the cardiac arrest patient first. Base camp out." Turning the dial back again, "Alicia and Eve to channel five." Switching the dial again. "Base camp to Alicia and Eve."

"A and E in the house." Alicia said, she loves cute nicknames and lingo when she's paired with someone.

"A and E, I need you on the casino floor. Need cardiac arrest patient transported to Valley View emergency room. No ETA for the coroner."

"Hear you loud and clear. A and E out." Eve spoke before turning the dial back to the main channel. I hear all the other conversations coming through from the various crew members on shift.

"Is it always this lit on a Tuesday?" Chris asked, I look over my shoulder at him. I see him pick up the mason jar off my desk and pull it onto his lap. "Saving up for that cruise? Thought you didn't want to go?"

I walk to my desk with my radio in hand. "I didn't but Stephanie already put a down payment on it. It'll be stupid to put that money to waste, won't it?"

"Yep, here." He said shifting about to pull out change from his pocket and drop it into the empty jar, "Change from my Uber here, that's got to help the account for something over the next six weeks."

"Thank you for the donation. You did ruin my surprise though."

"Surprise?" He asked with a perk of an eyebrow.

"I bought craft supplies to deck out your throne." I said dumping out the other bag of craft supplies and both of us burst into laughter.

"Shall I take the other chair so you can use your free time decorating?"

"With how today is going, no decorating will be done. You are going to be taking up my lunch break." I spoke. I start to navigate through things on my computer to get a little bit of work done before I need to wheel him down to the training facility. I exit all the programs and log off my computer before I stand up from my chair. I grasp my lunch bag to take with me. "Let's get to rolling."

"Are you going to be able to eat and drive this thing?"

"That's why you are going to hold my lunch. I will eat on my walk back across the casino." I said moving the wheelchair closer to him so he didn't have to move across the office. I set my bagged lunch in his lap as I took charge in rolling him out of the office. I pushed the chair through the casino to take him to the training facilities.

"Who packed your lunch?" He asked ruffling through the bag. "Sweet, Doritos!" He pulls the bag open and pops a chip into his mouth. I have never met this guy before, but I can't help but to laugh and roll my eyes at him. I should be mad at his actions but that's something Stephanie would do to me.

Chris is going to be routinely here until he heals. I will be learning who he is and what he's like. Thus far, I think that I'm digging him and think I can handle this short-term friendship. Lord knows, when he heals there won't be anything between us. "Who was the kid?"

"Kid?" I was confused about where that came from. Chris opens his mouth, pouring the crumbs from the bottom of the bag into his mouth.

"In the picture on your desk."

"Oh…he's my nephew." I answered when the elevator doors opened. I push him into the elevator shaft, turning him around to face the doors.

"Cute kid. Does he live with your mom? The other girl in the picture?"

"You can say that. My sister, his mom, died in childbirth." I said looking up at the monitor that showed the floors we were passing. I haven't discussed this with anyone since Xavier was born. Crystal doesn't even know the honest truth. Xavier is my son if anyone asks, and I wouldn't have it any other way. I also felt that I haven't given myself the proper time to grieve my sister's death. It's hard to grieve when Xavier reminds me of Meg in so many different ways that it's like she never died.

"I'm sorry for your loss, no wonder you haven't gone out and lived." He broke the awkward silence.

"What do you mean by that?"

"I'm an uncle myself, I spoil my nieces and nephews like crazy. I still have my sisters here to raise them, you don't. You are probably overprotective of that kid and probably helping your mom in more ways than one in raising him."

"Would you change your mind about me if I said I adopted him?" I asked nervously as he reached forward pushing a button on the elevator panel to get it to stop.

"No, it won't. It'll make me respect you more. Look, as a dude, having kids isn't always a deal breaker. I just met you and see how hard working you are, you need that cruise. If you have closed yourself off so much due to having the child in your life, you need to get out more. And don't get any ideas, you're most definitely not my type. And I'm all wrong for you." He said pushing the button again, getting us both to laugh.

"Then who is my type, my Obi-Wan-Kanobi?" I joked as the doors open and I pushed him out of the elevator.

"I can mingle around at work."

"Chris, I just have a fear that a guy will reject me because of my son."

"Nephew, technically, and if they reject you, then they are jerks."

18

"I think that's why I have been running scared, the fear of rejection." I admitted, not wanting to go into detail about the reasons why I had the fear and the reasons being my ex boyfriend, Dave.

"You have to live a little. You only have one life, sweet cheeks." He said with a wink before he pushed the automatic door button to allow him access into the training facility.

"Did you just call me sweet cheeks?" I asked with a chuckle.

"Yes, I did. See you in a few." He said with a wink. I stand there in shock as the door starts to close behind Chris, how in the heck did he figure me out after only meeting me twice? I turn on my heels and slowly walk back to my office completely defeated.

Am I that pathetic or am I that predictable? I plop down in my office chair and pull the picture frame to my lap. I think I am going to clock out early after picking Chris up to spend time with Xavier. When the hotel had me working these lengthy shifts, it was hard to spend any time with Xavier. Chris was right about one thing, we only had one life. I need to live a little and be a better mother.

I begin to review all the paperwork Stephanie and Crystal had done for me. After that, I begin to draw up all the proper paperwork for the events that occurred today. I have to wait to complete the forms until we get the reports back from all the participating parties. I try to find stuff to do to pass time until I have to head back to the training facility.

I climb off the elevator right when Chris is wheeling himself out the double doors. "Chris! How'd it go?"

"They didn't tell me anything new. They told me I tore my ACL and meniscus which is old news by now."

"What did you expect?"

"A miracle."

"Don't we all?" I joke. I push the button to get the elevator doors to reopen and steer him into the small room. "Chris, how'd you conclude all that about me earlier?"

"My sister was in a similar boat."

"How so?"

"She divorced when my nephew was two years old, she dived deep into work and focused on her son more than her own well being."

"How long?"

"How long until we kicked it out of her?"

"Yes."

"A few years when all of us got tired of seeing her miserable."

"Chris?" I ask, he looks up at me from his chair, "Do I seem miserable?"

Chris burst into laughter. After a few minutes, he calms down enough to be able to speak. "Ok, ok. I'm sorry. You seem overworked and lacking the love you deserve. You haven't given yourself enough self-love nor have had fun until I showed up, I'm sure." He cockily states, he is right that he has truly brightened my daily routine. "I think before this cruise, that's well deserved as it is, you should take some time to pamper yourself. You said yourself that this hotel is in debt to you so take some time to go wash out whatever box hair dye that is."

"This is my natural hair." I said offensively.

"My bad."

"Am I that hideous?"

"You're not that bad, you haven't met my friend Alex." He laughs at himself, and I roll my eyes.

"Now I'm a dude?"

"Aren't we all dudes? I call a lot of girl's dude. Maybe going on that single's cruise will be good for you. You aren't going to be meeting mister right looking like a fire hydrant in those hideous EMT outfits and pushing me around." Chris says as we both laugh. I look down at the yellow mustard attire that had multiple stains that have failed to come out over the years. "You might attract a dog, woof woof."

"You're ridiculous. Why am I nice to you?"

"Because you took pity on me." He says as he gives a pout and big puppy eyes, batting them even.

"As I should, because you're crippled."

"Ouch." He said with a chuckle.

"How much are all these Uber rides? How far do you live from the hotel?" I ask as I sit down on a bench next to him.

"Well, my sister is picking me up right now. Some of the guys may pitch in on rides. But they drop me off here so I don't make the journey from the parking lot."

"That seems fair. Well Chris, I'm off the clock. I'll see you tomorrow. You ok on your crutches until your sister gets here?"

"Yeah, I'm a big boy, mom."

"They grow up so quick on me." I said ruffling his hair some, "You need a haircut."

"Do not." He said sternly standing up with little assistance.

"If you say so."

"I expect my throne to be bedazzled by tomorrow lunchtime."

"I just said I'm off the clock, what makes you think I'll work on your throne?"

"Because you like me." He said with a half-smile. I roll my eyes pushing the chair back towards my office that is still empty, surprisingly. I write a note that I am taking the chair home with me, the hotel won't miss the chair for one night.

I head to my son's school to pick him up early. My mom is working late and I felt horrible sending her to take Xavier from school to daycare on her lunch break.

"Mom!!" Xavier exclaims when I walk into his class. Xavier runs up with his dinosaur in hand and wraps one arm around my waist. "You don't have work?"

"I left early, you want to go home and watch dinosaurs with pizza?" I ask as he nods excitedly. I sign him out before leading him to my run-down white Chevy Blazer. The exterior might be rough on the eyes and the check engine light may have been on for a couple months, but it gets me around this small, big town Las Vegas is.

I stop at Little Caesar's pizza grabbing dinner and a Redbox movie or two before the two-block drive home. Xavier runs to the bathroom to wash up while I make our plates. Xavier is obsessed with anything dinosaur so Jurassic Park is the movie choice for tonight. I feel Jurassic Park is too advanced for him, but he loves it. Xavier dives over the arm of the couch pulling the remote to his lap to turn on the movie.

I think Chris has done me well, he has given me an outsider's perspective on my life. He made me realize that everyone sees that I work hard and don't play harder. Xavier is growing up faster than grass, and I am letting it slip by. No more overtime, and my mom has picked up so much slack cause I have done such long shifts that it's not fair to her.

"When is hockey season starting again? Can we go to a Golden Knight game?" Xavier asks excitedly when he bites into his pizza.

"It starts next year, so we have to wait a few months." I say ruffling his hair as I set my plate on the coffee table. "Stay here babe, I have to get stuff from the car."

"Ok, mommy." Xavier says as I head into the garage where I parked this time around. I sent my mom a text that I picked Xavier up early from school and she could go home today if she wanted or crash here again. I grab the craft supplies and wheelchair heading back into the house. "Why'd you bring a wheelchair home, mom? You didn't have to bring work home with you, did you?" Xavier asked, peering over the back of the couch.

"No, an employee got a really bad boo boo. He needs a wheelchair for months. I'm going to decorate it for him."

"May I help? If it's for a boy, you need a boy's touch, mom. You're a girl."

"That I am, you want to come show me?" I ask as he slides off the couch. I grab our food and bring it to the dining room table so we can eat while we decorate.

"What's his name?"

"Chris."

"How do you spell that?" Xavier asked, pulling open a blue marker. I spell it out for him one letter at a time and watch him spell it sloppily on the decorated part of the chair. "There. Perfect. Mom, why are there no other boys in our house? I don't have a dad like the other kids."

"Because mom is too devoted to work to find a dad. We don't need a dad to be happy." I sighed ruffling his hair.

"Will I ever meet Chris? I want to meet him, so he knows who made this." Xavier said, looking up at me.

"He knows you already, he saw your picture on my desk."

"Well, I hope he likes it, mommy. He will love it and feel very happy."

"Yes, he will. He's been very upset that he is hurt."

"I don't like having boo-boos either." Xavier sighs before he cleans up his dinner plate for me. He goes to lay on the living room floor to watch the rest of the movie. I wheel the chair aside to dry from all the glue Xavier used, I sit at the table and pull my foot onto the chair with me. I unlock my iPhone to go through my contacts to text Chris that his throne is now bedazzled by a six-year-old boy. I then text my mom that I need her to babysit while I am on the cruise.

I click my phone off, I look over at Xavier, who is making two dinosaurs' fight. How am I going to go on a cruise? I know it is only for a few days, but I worry about being away from Xavier that long. I wasn't going to be five minutes away anymore when I'm at work, I am going to be sailing to Mexico from California. I still have to book my flight to California since I don't trust my car to make that journey.

I check my bank to see where I am financially and I think that I can swing everything. Work does have a lot of back pay they owe me; I have worked eighty plus hours every week since I got promoted two years ago and they can only pay out eighty hours every two weeks. I don't even have to use my PTO to go on the cruise and I'll still be paid for it. I just feel that my paychecks don't reflect the work I've put in.

Maybe I should start having fun and take myself seriously. *Box dyed hair.* I thought back to what Chris said. I grasped some of my hair and looked at it. I like my hair color, maybe I should get my nails done instead between now and the cruise. I want to look and feel good if I want to try to make a love connection. I just want to meet someone that will not only love me but will love and accept Xavier. I don't want Xavier to get attached to someone then we break up and leave Xavier absolutely devastated. It's not just me.

"Mommy?"

"Yeah?" I snap out of my thoughts.

"May we have ice cream?"

"Oh, yeah…" I said standing up to dish out ice cream for both of us. I sit on the couch eating my bowl of ice cream as Xavier is playing with his set of dinosaurs.

"Xavier, before we start bath time may I get a picture of you with your masterpiece?" I ask as I look at the now dried wheelchair. Xavier gets up running over to the wheelchair with his favorite dinosaur, that he named Gary, in tow. I snap a picture with my phone texting it over to Chris, hopefully he'll get a kick out of it. Being an uncle, I am sure he's great with kids.

"Could Gary take a bath with me?"

"Yes, but he can't get wet because he'll be damaged." I explain as he nods. I go to the bathroom to draw his bath while Xavier goes to his room to get ready for bath. Once I get him settled in the bath, I leave the door open while I get his school bag, both lunches and everything ready for the next day. "Mom! I'm done!" Xavier shouts out from the bathroom. I put our bagged lunches in the refrigerator to keep cool overnight before I go to assist Xavier. Xavier holds the towel tightly closed around his body while he walks to his bedroom to get dressed while I clean up the bathroom. I walk to check on Xavier who is sitting on his bed playing with his Batman action figures. "Why doesn't Batman come to Vegas?"

"Because Gotham is full with crime, he doesn't have time to come here." I sigh out as I sit on the edge of his bed. Xavier crawls up his bed and slides under his dinosaur comforter.

"Where is Gotham?"

"In Arkansas." I respond when I feel my phone vibrate. I pull out my phone seeing Chris sent me a selfie of himself doing a thumbs up. "Chris loves your work, he gave you a thumbs up."

"Really?" Xavier asks diving out of his blanket to land on my lap to look at my phone. He looks at the selfie of Chris giving a thumbs up. "Is he happy?"

"Very happy."

"How'd you meet him, mommy?"

"I was there to help him when he got hurt." I respond as he slides back under his blanket. "You want a story about Gary?"

"Please? I love when you make up stories about Gary and my adventures." He says with giggles and smiles.

Chapter Three:

Six Weeks Later-

I lean back in my office chair staring at the half empty mason jar on my desk. My flight to California is tomorrow morning. The jar is nowhere near where it needs to be to finish funding this trip. I had punched a lot of numbers over the last few weeks trying to figure out if this trip is even financially possible. If I could fill this jar one last time by the end of my shift that I could make this trip financially possible.

I sigh, I am already mentally preparing myself that I won't be going. I am already planning out what to say when I go to call Stephanie and bail at the last minute. Stephanie left early due to it being so slow and she was pumped to go on the cruise. The cruise was all she wanted to discuss. I didn't want to think of the cruise because I am beyond upset that I won't be going.

"The party is here." Chris' booming voice erupts in the room. I look up at the door seeing him standing in the doorway.

"I'm surprised you're here. Thought you had that cruise." I said tossing my pen softly onto my desk.

"Alex and I are driving out to California tonight after my doctor's appointment; I need to grab some things from the locker room. What's with the long face?" He asks as he plops down into his designated wheelchair without any help and wheels himself over to my desk.

"I can't go on my cruise. How do I break this to Stephanie?"

"What? You have to go." He said in pure shock.

"Funds."

"Ten four to base camp." I hear over the radio.

"Base camp here, what's the status?" I ask moving to the cork board to look at all the schedules.

"We have an asthma attack in progress at the venue. Transporting to the ambulance bay."

"Alex and Aiden are on deck. Ten four." I said, setting my receiver back down on its charger. I figure it can charge up while I take Chris down to the arena. I turn around to see Chris shifting in his seat. "Not comfortable? I thought your butt was already imprinted in that chair."

"Oh, it is." Chris said with a big smile. I go to my desk to grab my lunch pail so I can eat on the walk back. As I squat down to grab the pail from under my desk, my eyes land on the mason jar that now has a wad of cash inside it.

"Wait, where did all that money come from?" I ask confused.

"Me. I hope that covers it." He says, staring down at his lap, not wanting to make eye contact with me. I pull out the cash and toss it onto his lap.

"I can't Chris, you've already donated enough."

Chris tosses the wad of cash back onto the desk, "You're going."

"Make me." I said sternly and put my hands on my hips.

"Tara, you, and I both know you want to go. You have been

counting down the minutes until your flight. You deserve it. Please? Consider this a tip and for all the bags of chips I have jacked and continue to jack from your lunch."

"Are you sure, Chris?"

"Positively sure, I probably owe you that amount just in all the chips I have ate of yours." He said that was the sweetest gesture ever. I look at the cash and try not to cry from happiness. I walk around my desk hugging him the best I can. "What time is your flight?"

"I leave in the morning. I should call it an early day."

"Well, let's make this quick." He said with a smirk. I wheel him out of the office, and towards the training facility.

"I can't believe you're going on a cruise crippled."

"Wouldn't you?"

"Aren't you afraid?"

"Of what? My biggest fear is that I'm stuck with Alex all weekend."

"When do I meet Alex? You keep bashing him like he's the plague or something." I said walking backwards onto the elevator before pulling him onto the shaft with me.

"He's like me. But worse."

"I doubt that. But no wonder he's your partner in crime."

"I guess."

"Well, if you won't be long, I'll stay here." I said as I push the blue square to get the automatic doors to open for him. I lean against the wall, pulling out my phone to distract me while I wait for Chris. The doors open again moments later, Chris was wheeling himself through the double doors with a duffel bag on his lap.

"Told you that it'll be quick."

"That you did, let me wheel you out front so I can get going."

"Are you going to dump me and run? You at least owe me that bag of chips." He spoke. I roll my eyes, but he is right. I owe him that bag of chips since he paid for it already. I set my lunch on his lap and he begins to shuffle through the lunch pulling out the chips, "Score! Cheetos!" I roll my eyes as he eats the whole bag during the walk to the taxi line.

The Next Morning-

I am in my bedroom throwing the last-minute items into my suitcase trying to prepare for my flight. I am waiting on Stephanie to come pick me up, my mother is supposed to be here any minute to pick Xavier up. My phone begins to ring, I pick up my cell phone seeing Stephanie's picture and name shining on the screen. I quickly answer it when Xavier runs in carrying his two dinosaurs making 'roaring' noises.

"Stephanie, where are you?" I ask planting the phone between my ear and shoulder.

"I can't go this weekend, sorry Tara." Stephanie said.

"What do you mean you can't go?"

"I'm sick with the flu, you can still go."

"No, it's fine. Feel better and call me if you need anything." I was a little upset because I was looking forward to a weekend with my best friend. This weekend was going to be without work or worrying about my son. I love Xavier, but it would be nice to spend a weekend without the responsibility that came with being a parent. I hang up tossing the phone onto the bed and drag my hands along my face not sure what to do now. I have the whole weekend off, maybe I can plan things with Xavier? What can I do with Xavier?

"When are you leaving mommy?" Xavier asked.

"I'm not, Aunt Stephanie is sick so mommy can't go." I answered.

"Why can't you go? She's sick and you can go by yourself." He said when the doorbell rang, "Grandma is here!" He yells jumping off my bed causing my heart to skip a beat. He runs out of the room, and I am close behind him. Xavier opens the door, my mom stands on the front porch. "Grandma!" He exclaimed. My mom squats down with open arms; Xavier runs into her arms giving her a big hug. My mom wraps her arms around Xavier's small frame picking him up with her.

"Have you been good, Xavier?" My mom asked, with me not working over time my mom hasn't been needed to help with watching him.

"Yes! I got a new dinosaur set!" He said showing my mom the dinosaur he was holding; he must have dropped the other dinosaur that came in the set.

"I see that. Why don't you go get your bags?" My mom asks, setting Xavier down.

"Why do I need my bags?" Xavier asked.

"I'm not going, Stephanie is sick." Filling my mom in on the news.

"Just because she's sick doesn't mean you can't go...it's a cruise and it's already paid for. You worked so hard to pay it off and it'll be a waste. I drove the hour in traffic, mind you, to be here to get Xavier. " My mom said.

"It won't be fun going alone." I said.

"That's why it's a single's cruise so you can meet other people."

"I don't know." I turn around, running a hand through my hair. My mom came into the house shutting the door behind her.

"Mom, you can take me." Xavier said as my mom and I chuckle.

"You're a little too young there, buddy." I said.

"You should go mommy; it'll be fun. Grandma will watch me, and we will play with dinosaurs and Batman."

"Yeah Tara, just go. It can be fun and if it's not, then you can blame us." My mom said.

"Fine, I'll go. I have thirty minutes to get to the airport to catch my flight." Messing with my watch after checking the time. I go into my room, zip my suitcase shut and grab my purse. Seeing Xavier sitting on my mom's lap telling her stories from school and all about this new friend he had made.

"Do you want me to give you a ride so you don't have to pay for parking? My mom offered.

"If you don't mind." I say as my mom sets Xavier down to grab her keys. We walk out to her car putting Xavier in his booster seat. My mom buckles Xavier in while I am putting my suitcase in the trunk. I pray that my mom can get me there on time.

My mom drives us over to the airport, pulling up to the drop off area and that is when I begin to get nervous. I have never been on a plane before and now I am going on one by myself. I climb out of the car and lean in to speak to my son, "Behave, Xavier. I love you."

"I love you too, mommy. Have fun and buy me a souvenir." Xavier said with a smile. I grab my luggage, standing there dumbfounded. I am stranded at the airport so there is no turning back. I am going on this cruise whether I want to or not.

I went into the airport to check into my flight and hand over my luggage. The flight was quick, my nerves amplified because it is delayed which makes me worry that I will miss the boat. I flag down a taxi to take me over to the harbor. The taxi pulls up to the harbor with minutes to spare so I beeline onto the giant cruise ship not to be left behind.

I take a deep breath and find a map of the ship to find where I am to check in. As I am on my way to the check-in area, I keep seeing giant posters that have half-naked men, very few women who have a little more clothes on, with the words 'Pure Gold' written at the bottom.

"I didn't know this cruise would have strippers." I say out loud, but it is soft enough for no one else to hear it. I spot a poster with a guy that has to be in his 50's or 60's, "Ew, I do NOT want to see that…" I say grossed out and keep walking to find the line to check in. I wait in line texting Stephanie that I went on the cruise without her and hope she didn't mind. I put my phone on silent for the remainder of the day and my mom knew not to call me unless it was an emergency.

My mom is the same person that wanted me to go because she wants me to get married. I am kind of iffy about this whole cruise. I look around seeing a lot of men, not very many women and a lot more kids than I thought there would be. Why bring kids on a singles cruise? How would you have kids if you're single? I have no room to talk, but mine is a different story.

Maybe this is a LGBTQ cruise for singles? Explains why there are more men strippers than female strippers.

"I'm going to kill Stephanie." I said not believing I fell for this. But hey, some of those strippers are good looking. Gay or not, I can still enjoy watching them do their thing. I try to entertain myself as I walk through the line. I am called up to the counter to an associate, his eyebrows are pinched, his whole posture is tense, and he barely acknowledges that I am there.

"How may I help you?" He asked.

"Are you okay? You seem kind of tense." I said as he just now looks up at me from the paperwork in front of him.

"Well, we put someone in one room, and now he can't be in that room. He broke his leg so he needs a handicap accessible room. We don't have any more left unless we push out a family." He explained.

"I was a party of two and I'm now a party of one. If it helps any, you can move me about." I said trying to be helpful and understand how that can be stressful.

"What name is it under?"

"It'll be under my friend's name, Stephanie Ortiz."

"You aren't Stephanie, you're Tara." He looks up at me from the computer monitor.

"Yep." I nodded.

"Let me see." He was nodding, mumbling under his breath and typing away at the computer, "Okay, I can move you here and move this family here and move him here."

"Everything figured out?"

"Yep, you're in room 4873." He said more relaxed than before. He shuffled about giving me a key and printing out receipts for me.

"Thanks." I said smiling before I grabbed my things. I followed the map he gave me trying to find the way to my room. I climb onto an elevator going up to the fourth floor and walk down the hallway that looks out over the shopping mall below.

I see a man who piques my interest walking towards me. He has to be an inch or two taller than me, he wears his jacket zipped up to his neck and his hood flipped up like he is trying to blend in. Why he is trying to blend in, I don't know.

I keep glancing at him trying to make out any or all the possible features that I can. We slide past each other in the open concept hallway. A few steps later, I notice his wallet laying on the ground.

I bend down to pick it up and turn around, "HEY!" I yell to get his attention. The man turns around to look at me, "You dropped this!" Holding the wallet up in visible site. I run up to him, leaving my suitcase where it was to return the wallet to him.

"Thanks." He said. When I am finally standing in front of him, I am able to make out the brightest smile. He has the most beautiful hazel eyes and dark hair that is barely falling out from the hood. He starts to push the hair out of his face.

"No problem." Smiling back at him. I turn back around to head back to my suitcase. I continue to search for my room that has to be on this floor somewhere.

I find my room and let myself in. I walk in, shutting the door behind me and lock it so others can't get in. I leave my suitcase at the door.

"I have a connecting room. You're being locked because I don't want whoever it is letting themselves in." I said out loud. I lock the deadbolt. I look at the single bed that has a dark blue comforter tucked in under the mattress. My eyes continue to scan the room seeing the standard nightstand, dresser with television planted on it and a small closet cove.

I spot a small circular window with silver trim with the perfect view of the endless ocean, "Ocean view, not bad." I shrug before I go to check out the bathroom amenities. The room was definitely going to be comfortable to live in for the next few days. I collect my personal hygiene items from my luggage and carry them into the bathroom when I hear banging coming from one of the doors.

"Open the door!" I hear a man yell; I begin to feel my body tense up and become tingly with a sense of panic. I step in front of my main door, pressing my hands against the door for support as I look through the peephole. No one was there. I slowly twirl around to look at the connecting door.

Banging comes from the door again, "Just open the dang door, Chris." The man said. My hand nervously shakes, raising it to grasp the metal tab turning it. Everything seems to be in slow motion. The lock clicks when it unlocks. My whole body quivering a little unsure what is going to happen next when I open the purplish-blue door.

On the opposite side of the door stands the man that had dropped his wallet. He stands there facing me but this time, he isn't wearing his hood tightened around his long face. He has a little bit of scruff; his jet-black hair falls just above his ear and half his head is freshly shaved with a fade. He wore a leather jacket with metal studs on the collar, his jacket was unbuttoned to expose the black hoodie underneath. His dark denim jeans were on the tighter side. A metal chain hooking onto his belt loops. He has this complete rock star vibe about him, I bite at my bottom lip because I am instantly attracted to him physically.

"Whoa, you're not Chris."

"No, I'm not Chris." I said with a bit of a nervous chuckle, "I'm Tara. I guess we are going to be neighbors this weekend." I continue. I stick my hand out hoping to shake his hand. He went to grab my hand when the boat jerks sharply. The sudden movement causes both of us to stumble. I fell forward into his embrace. Luckily, he is stronger than me and catches me before I fall face first into the ground. "I'm so sorry." I say embarrassed as he helps me back to my feet.

"No problem, sweetie. I'm Alex." He says with a half smile.

"Hi, Alex. Sorry about taking your friend's room. There were some issues at check in. Something about a man breaking his leg or something and this room not being handicap accessible."

"Yep, that would be Chris." Alex said, nodding.

"I know a Chris who has a bad leg, but he's on a different cruise."

"Small world." He said.

"Well, it was nice to meet you." I say, I turn around to go back into my room and try to close the door behind me. Alex walks into the room with me, as much as I thought it was rude it just reminded me of Chris.

"What is a girl like you doing on a cruise by themselves?" He asked, looking over my room layout.

"What makes you think I'm here by myself?" I asked offensively, putting my hands on my hips.

With a chuckle, he said "The fact you took a room with one bed. If you came with someone else, you would have a spare bed. So, I'm assuming you're single considering the circumstances."

"Isn't everyone on this cruise single?" I asked with a blush that I got called out. I turn to look at him while I am pulling out things from my luggage. I hear a phone ringing and know it isn't mine due to the ring tone being a heavy rock song.

"Chris is calling, I got to go. It was nice meeting you, Tara. Will I catch you later?"

"You will see me around considering we are neighbors for

the next few days." I said smiling.

"True." He said as he walked through the connecting doors. I close mine and lock it before I finish unpacking my things.

I decide to go out and explore the boat. I keep seeing more posters for these strippers. I even see a poster that had a guy that looked just like Alex on it. I stop in my tracks staring up at it. He is wearing a pair of black shorts with random patches that look like the ones you could buy from Hot Topic and iron on. His hair fell to the side like how it was earlier. He was wearing the same leather jacket but with nothing underneath. His upper body was exposed seeing he had a six pack abs with a chiseled chest.

My neighbor is one of the strippers. I fell for a stripper. Great. I look at the other man in the poster who oddly looks identical to Chris from my work. *If that is Chris from my job, I knew he wrestled but didn't realize he stripped on his off time.* I thought more about it as I walk past the poster not wanting to stare at the poster anymore. I am afraid that having images of Alex shirtless burnt in my mind would make it hard for me to talk with him.

I grab some food before finding my way back to my room. I sit on my bed eating my food and watch whatever I can find interesting on the television. I set my lunch down and pull the agenda onto my lap. I read over the agenda for the weekend, none of it made sense to me. How were any of these scheduled events related to being single? Family Feud? Questions and answers with the superstars? Matches? Where was the speed dating or dances?

Chapter Four:

I hear a knock at the door. I check my main door, and the coast was clear. It must be Alex again. I walk over to the connecting door, pull it open and allow Alex into my room.

"Are you a stripper?" I asked blatantly. He gave me a questionable look like I was drunk.

"What?" He asks with a chuckle.

"Are you a stripper?" I asked dead serious.

"No! Why? Do I look hot enough to be one?" He asked, shaking out his black hair. I look him up and down again. I bite at my lip liking what I see but don't want to honestly answer that.

"I'm not going to answer that." I turn around walking further into my room with him on my heel. "I could have sworn I saw a picture of you hanging down in the mall area."

"Well, that is good and all because that was me in that picture."

"So, you are a stripper?" I said turning around and pointed at him in an aha moment.

"Am I missing something about my life that I need to know about?" Alex asked with another chuckle.

"Apparently. This is a single's cruise and the people in the posters are strippers." I said confidently, taking a few steps towards my bed. I stop to turn to look at Alex, beginning to doubt myself, "Aren't they?"

He burst into laughter, "You have been lied to."

"What do you mean I've been lied to?" I gasp in shock.

"This isn't a single's cruise," He said between laughs and shaking his head no, "This is a wrestling cruise."

"Wrestling? You're a wrestler?" I was more shocked.

"Yeah, you didn't know?"

"No, my friend booked the cruise. I'm going to kill her." I said turning around smacking my forehead with my palm. I felt completely stupid at the moment.

This weekend is not going to be fun; I don't even watch wrestling. I guess now will be the time to start and since the casino has the training facility. Maybe it will give me a reason to go support the wrestlers there. But who am I kidding? I don't have time between work and Xavier. I only go down there to escort Chris.

"It isn't that bad. Come on, we have the emergency procedure video to watch in the banquet room and I have to pick Chris up."

"Your tag partner?"

"And my best friend." Alex added.

"Right." I nod. I grab my belongings before I follow him out of the room.

"Do you watch wrestling?"

"Honestly?" I ask as I give him a side glance.

"Honestly, I won't get offended."

"No. But I do watch hockey if that is any better."

"Who is your favorite team?" Alex asked as we wait for the elevator to arrive.

"The Golden Knights, they are my home team." I said.

"So, you live in Vegas? "

"Born and raised." I answered, "What about yourself?"

"Born in Michigan, have a house there along with sharing an apartment in Vegas since my work has me there."

"You travel a lot being a wrestler?" I ask curiously as we climb onto the elevator shaft.

"Rarely, but it does happen. The only traveling I do is from Michigan to Vegas. Maybe I'll stay in Vegas more if that is where you are."

"Stalker?" I asked jokingly.

"Do I look like the stalking type?" Alex asks as I look him up and down.

"Can't any of us be a stalking type?"

"Not a truer statement." Alex said as it went quiet, and the elevator-tinged symbolizing we were at the bottom floor. Alex let me walk off first and he led me towards Chris's room. "Your friend told you this was a single's cruise?"

"Yeah, don't ask. Please?" I beg.

"I was right when I came to the conclusion that you were single."

"Maybe." I said blushing a little. Alex stopped in front of a door, but I didn't. I bump right into him. My face begins to burn from embarrassment that I almost took him out for the second time today, "I'm so sorry."

"It's fine, tall people like us don't stop suddenly. How tall are you? 5'8ish?"

"Yes, how do you do that?"

"I have a measuring eye." Alex says with a wink. Without even knocking, the door bangs open.

"About time, Alex." Chris says with agitation, his eyes finally landing on me. "Tara? What are you doing here?" Chris asked, confused. He isn't the only one confused. My head snapped to see the same Chris from work.

"You know Chris?" Alex asked, looking at me shocked.

"Yeah, this is the Chris I knew who had a bad leg that I told you about." I said.

"If you know him through work, how did you not know he was a wrestler?"

"I knew he wrestled, but I didn't know this was the wrestling cruise he was going on." I said. Chris is darting his eyes between us confused as to what is going on and why we are together, I'm sure. Wanting to change the subject, I look to Chris "What did the doctor say about your leg?"

"I have another three months until I can get a walking brace, it didn't heal properly based on the MRI." He said leaning forward against the crutches.

"She thought we were strippers." Alex said with a laugh and tried to jump into the conversation.

"You thought we were strippers?" Chris asked, shocked.

"I hate you two." I said turning to walk away with my head hung low. An announcement came over to remind everyone about reporting to the banquet room for the emergency procedure review.

"Tara! Wait for us! I can only move so fast." Chris yells. I stop only to wait for Chris because I feel bad for him. I thought he would need help with his leg being the way it is. "I told you she will slow down, she's a worry wart."

"Am not, Chris." I huff. I help him down the stairs, walking beside him to the banquet room. I am looking over the crowd that has already formed, it is mixed with people that I can tell are wrestlers and those who aren't. I approach the last row where Chris plops himself into the aisle seat. I grab the two metal crutches from Chris carrying them to rest them against the wall. "I'm going to set your crutches here. I wonder if they have any wheelchairs for you to use."

"Oh yeah, a wheelchair will be so much safer on a ship. I will be randomly rolling around due to the currents." Chris said with a roll of his eyes.

"You want to hobble around this big cruise ship?"

"Maybe." Chris said.

"You're so weird Chris…" I said, rolling my eyes this time.

"I'm weird? I'm only grateful you took the room next to Alex, he's just as weird."

"I bet." I said with a chuckle. I start to remember all these jabs and one-liners Chris has said about Alex over the last few weeks. Chris spoke so much of this Alex guy and now I am stuck with him.

"You have no idea." Chris said smiling when Alex approached us with pamphlets. He begins to hand us each a pamphlet that he has in hand. Alex grabs my hand and leads me to a row closer to the front.

"Why are we sitting up here? I thought you would want to sit with Chris?" I was confused why we weren't going to sit with Chris, I thought he would want to sit with his best friend. I slide into the third row and claim the empty seat next to him.

"I have bad eyesight and I didn't bring my glasses." He answers as I notice how close he has the paper held to his face. I try to imagine what glasses would look like on him, why do I think he'll still be sexy as heck in glasses? Why am I already calling him sexy?

"If you and Chris work together, how come I never seen you?" I ask.

"I can ask the same thing about you." Alex says with a glance.

"Are all these people wrestlers?" I ask, looking at the people sitting around us.

"Not all of them." Alex answer as he looks up at the stage. "There are fans on here too."

"How does this wrestling cruise work?" I was intrigued when speaking came over the sound system.

"I have no idea. I'm just here." He said with a shrug. I burst into laughter, "What?"

"You are a wrestler, on the wrestling cruise, but you don't know what there is to do?"

"I just know that I have a few matches to do, a Q&A and a meet and greet."

"That explains the agenda."

"Why is a girl like you single?" Alex asked, it was a bit of a jump in conversation. I am hesitant to answer because I wasn't sure if I should tell him the truth or not. I look over my shoulder at Chris, Chris knows the truth. He didn't seem to care that I was mother. Alex followed my eye, "You like Chris? He is quite handsome."

Alex's voice seems sad compared to normal and he shifts in his seat like he is uncomfortable at the idea that I like his best friend. I burst into laughter. "No, thank you."

"So, you don't like him? What's your story then? You come on a singles cruise so you must have been desperate." Alex said shifting in his seat to look at me better. We weren't even giving the safety presentation any attention.

"My friend signed me up because she felt I was miserable

without a guy."

"Are you?" He asked with a perked brow. I open my mouth to answer when everyone begins to clap. The presentation was already over?

"I need to help Chris." I swiftly stand up and go to retrieve the crutches for Chris. We follow the crowds outside to the various boats that we are to use in the event of a rescue mission. We stand in the back while Chris hobbles to find a place to sit.

"Besides hockey, do you watch any other sport?" Alex asked, I'm so glad he changed the subject and could tell I didn't want to talk about it.

"Sometimes baseball."

"You will be watching wrestling after this weekend."

"Will I?" I asked Alex with a perked brow.

"It will pull you in."

"Will it pull me in, or will you pull me in?"

"A little bit of both." Alex said with a wink and smile.

"I hate boats." I said as the boat rocked a tad and I grip onto my pants tightly, unsure what that would do.

"If you don't like boats, why go on one?"

"I thought cruise ships were different and I haven't been on one since my sister almost drowned." I lie, it really happened to Xavier.

"How does your sister drowning involve a boat?" Alex asked.

"She jumped overboard and she almost drowned." I lie.

"I can see how that can be scary. What's the age difference?"

"Oh, the age difference?"

"How do you not know the age difference between you and your sister?"

"We are four years apart." I answered, it has been years since I had to answer or even discuss things related to my sister. I haven't wanted to talk about her, I feel that I haven't been able to fully grieve her loss. I had to instantly become a mom and didn't have the time to think about it.

"Not that much of a difference." Alex said.

"Do you have any siblings?"

"Nope, only child. I look to Chris as a brother from another mother."

"I look to my best friend like that. We have been best friends since kindergarten, so we have grown up together." I said.

"She's the one that was supposed to be here?"

"Yep."

"What a witch. You don't leave a sister hanging like that."

"She has the flu."

"Oh, then that is fine. We don't like the flu near us."

"I bet." I said, chuckling a tad from his facial reaction. Alex and I aren't paying attention to the instructions we are being given about how to use the rescue boats. I just hope that there won't be any emergencies during this trip because we will both be goners for sure.

Chapter Five:

I turn around to walk over to where Chris had found to sit. I want to help Chris back to his room, maybe it was my professional side coming out but I want to make sure that Chris didn't get injured any more. Alex walks beside me, I am walking between the two men towards Chris's room.

"You took my old room?" Chris asked.

"Yeah, I got the connecting room next to Alex. He thought I was you earlier and that is how we met." I said.

"Like we weren't going to meet any other way." Alex said.

"Yeah, she would have met you while you were working that pole later." Chris joked with a hearty laugh.

"Will I ever live that down?" I asked, putting my hands on my hips.

"No, you won't. I got some moves, watch this!" Alex exclaimed. He hooks himself onto a pole and begins to grind against it. I cover my face blushing and keep walking. "Aw, push it...push it real good..." Alex starts singing while he dances.

"Go Alex, go Alex, go! Where are my dollars?" Chris asks as he is trying to dance on his crutches.

"You guys are ridiculous! Come on, Chris." I said, trying to grab him and help him to his room.

"Tara…Tara…" Alex said as he is walking and thrusting behind me. I begin to speed walk to get out of his path, but he keeps following me.

"Leave me alone! Alex, stop it! Alex!" I said, swatting at him. Chris has to stop and stand still because he is laughing so hard. Chris's face is turning as red as a tomato from how hard he is laughing.

"Am I sexy now?" Alex asked as he begins lifting his shirt up to expose the defined six pack abs and chiseled chest.

"Don't!" I said covering my face from embarrassment. He grabs me, wrapping his strong arms around my waist picking me up a tad, "Put me down!" I said kicking while Chris is trying to catch up.

"Alex Johnson! Put that poor girl down!" An older man said sternly.

"Yes, Mr. Henry." Alex said, relaxing his grip on me.

"Whoa!" I exclaim out as I fall from his grip and land flat on my butt.

"Oh my god! I'm so sorry! Are you okay?" Alex said, realizing that he just dropped me flat on my butt.

"I'm fine." I said slowly getting back to my feet with his help. I begin to dust myself off and trying not to blush from embarrassment because I had just fallen.

"Do I know you?" Mr. Henry asked.

"I'm Tara. I'm in the room next to Alex and I know Chris from work." I explained. I only hope that I wasn't going to get them in trouble.

"They aren't harassing you, are they? They are our most rambunctious tag team." He said as he pointedly glared between the two men that stand on either side of me.

"Oh yes, Chris is so rambunctious. With his broken leg and all. He's running amuck on this ship." I said with a laugh.

"You caught me. When you're not looking, I'm running all around like a mad dog." Chris said.

"A mad dog?" Alex asked with a chuckle.

"Yeah, a mad dog, gr!" Chris said.

"Okay. Well, Alex, you have a match with Kendrick in an hour. You need to go get suited up." Mr. Henry said.

"Will do." Alex nodded.

"Nice meeting you Tara, and thanks for coming onto the cruise." He said as Alex and Chris burst into laughter.

"Shut up you two." I said nudging them both.

"I don't want to know." Mr. Henry says before he waves his hand. He turns and goes on his way.

"I can walk Chris back to his room if you want to go get ready for your match." I said.

"Will you come watch?" Alex asked in a hopeful manner.

"I'll think about it." I said with a smile. Alex smiles back at me before he walks towards the elevators while I escort Chris back to his room.

"You know you don't have to help me; I'm a grown man." He says as I grab the crutches from him after he sat on his bed. Chris maneuvers himself up the bed and props his bum leg up on some pillows.

"I know, but I want to help. It's part of my job to take care of you."

"We aren't at work, which means you don't have to."

"I want to, I like helping." I said with a reassuring smile. I lean his crutches against the wall near his bed in case he needs them.

"I feel bad if you base your whole vacation around me."

"I won't base it around you, but by the looks of it my weekend will be anyway." I said.

"Don't be afraid to tell Alex no. He deserves to hear no once in a while." Chris said, chuckling.

"I will keep that in mind. I'm in room 4873 so feel free to call my room, do you still have my cell phone number?"

"Yeah, I still have your cell number."

"Okay, so if you can't get a hold of me in my room, call my cell and I will be around."

"Thanks Tara." Chris said smiling.

"Do you need anything?"

"Nope, I'm fine here." He said, smirking.

"Alright, I'm going to head back to my room." I said, patting his upper leg before I head out of his room to go up to my own room.

I try to get used to the small sway of the boat, but it is hard. I walk into my room, laying flat on my bed hoping that laying down will be better. Laying down, I can feel the swaying more dominantly which had made me feel ill. I laid there holding my stomach hoping the nausea feeling would go away, but it didn't.

I got up from my bed and went to my bathroom. I knelt beside the toilet, continuing to hold my stomach until I vomited. I sat beside the toilet bowl, leaning back against the wall and hope I don't have to vomit again. I stay in that position because I still feel as if I am going to be sick.

I can't help but to think about Alex. I wanted to go down and see his match, but I don't want to risk leaving this position

50

in my current condition. I sit here for Lord knows how long until a door opens, I knew it must be Alex.

"Tara?" Alex's voice is soft and filled with curiosity.

"I'm in here." I said loudly as I see Alex step into the doorway moments later. Concern spreads across his face and he pretty much runs into the room. He kneels down beside me with a hand falling to rest on my thigh while his beautiful hazel eyes meet mine.

"Are you okay?" He asked, concerned.

"I don't feel so well. I think I may be seasick." I sheepishly said, I knew that I was blushing due to the heat coming to my cheeks.

"What do you want me to do?"

"Is there a store on this ship?" I asked.

"This isn't a time to go shopping."

"Not that type of shopping." I said trying to get up on my own. He helps me get to my feet before he scoops me up into a fireman hold and carries me to the main room where he lays me down on the bed.

"What type of shopping?"

"I need to get something to make me feel better." I said as I reach for my wallet that is in my purse.

"Don't worry, I got it." Alex said, grasping my wrist. He makes sure I am situated before he hurries out of the room. I lay down on the bed trying to stay still. A half hour later, Alex returns to our rooms carrying a brown bag filled with things.

"Alex, what the heck did you get?" I asked, propping myself up on my elbows. I begin to regret my decision to have him get me medicine.

"I didn't know what you needed." Alex said as he starts to pull out the first item from the bag. A pack of pads, I start to blush and roll my eyes.

"I'm seasick, not on my period." I said. Alex tosses the pads over his shoulder without a care where they land. He reaches into the bag of mystery items and pulls out a pregnancy test, "I'm not pregnant."

"It's not funny, I don't know what you need. I even called Chris for help."

"Did he say to get all this?"

"No."

"Then why'd you get it?" I asked, chuckling.

"I wanted to be on the safe side." Alex said as he pulls out Pepto Bismuth, "I know this works for upset stomachs." He said as he sits it down on my bed.

"I'm curious what else you got."

"I got some ginger ale, crackers, and Dramamine patches." Alex said as he pulls them out.

"How much was all this?" I ask as I reach for my wallet to grab some cash.

"Don't worry about it, I want my buddy to feel better."

"Buddy?"

"Yep, you're my ship buddy for the weekend." He says with a smirk and a quick wink. He pulls the plastic off the Pepto bottle. With a quick twist of his wrist, the cap comes off and he pours the thick pink liquid into the clear cup to the measuring line. He hands over the medicine to me and I down it like a shot.

After I clear every drop, I hand it back to Alex. Alex walks into the bathroom to rinse out the cup. I grab the box of patches that are resting on the bed beside me. I rip open the box and slap a patch onto my arm in hopes it will start working before tomorrow.

I was embarrassed to be like this in front of Alex, the one guy that I PROBABLY had a shot with and now he has to take care of me. Alex comes back out, setting the Pepto aside. I wipe at my face, chuckling a tad. "What are you laughing at?"

"I'm embarrassed and when I get embarrassed, I tend to laugh." I explained.

"There isn't anything to be embarrassed about." Alex says as he moves the ginger ale so he can sit on the bed beside me.

"Yes, there is. A person my age shouldn't be seasick."

"A person my age shouldn't be afraid of sick people."

"You're afraid of sick people?"

"Afraid may not be the right word, I get uncomfortable around them. I worry too much about their well-being."

"As most people do." I said smiling.

"You want to split some ginger ale with me? We have a whole bottle here. It may not be as good as wine, or beer for that matter but it's still good." He said pulling the ginger ale bottle out from behind his back.

"Sounds good." I said with a smile. He goes to the bathroom to grab the complimentary cups that are on the sink. "How was your match?" I asked curiously as he hands over a cup to pull the plastic off of.

"It was good. I have had better matches, but it went well. No one got injured so that is always good." Alex said as I was finally able to remove the plastic from the cup.

"That's a good sign when no one gets injured."

"It is." Alex said, opening the ginger ale. I hold the two plastic cups while he pours the ginger ale, "Is that enough?"

"Yeah, I'm not a big ginger ale fan so less is better."

"You were the type of kid that never wanted to drink or eat what is best for them when they were sick."

"Yep, I was the kid that wanted to go out and play even if I was sick as a dog." I say as he places the ginger ale bottle on the nightstand and moves the box of crackers.

"Scoot over." Alex said all while shoving me. I begin scooting over to give him room to climb onto the bed next to me. He grabs the remote to turn the television on and flips it to the channel that was designated for Pure Gold wrestling matches.

"Who are those guys?" I notice the two big men in the ring.

"The red head is Chuck and the other is Matt Anthony."

"They're huge." I said sipping my ginger ale.

"And I'm not?"

"Sorry Alex, but they got some height and muscles on you." I said, smirking.

"Psh, whatever." Alex said, rolling his eyes. He was instructing me about each move and the technique behind it. I slowly lay down; my head propped up on his arm. "Are you feeling any better?" Alex asked after a few hours of watching these wrestling matches. He places the back of his other hand on my forehead, I look up to him smiling.

"Yeah, a tad."

"Your head is a little warm, I'll go get a wet washcloth." Alex says, I sit up so he can climb off the bed.

"You're a good Mr. Mom." I said chuckling.

"Well, you know." Alex said with a shrug. He went into the bathroom and came back with a drained washcloth and rests it over my forehead. He climbs onto the bed with me, I slowly fall asleep without knowing that I fell asleep on Alex's arm.

Chapter Six:

The next morning, I woke up from the feeling of something moving under my head. My eyes fluttered open to see Alex staring back at me. His eyes have dark bags under them and seem like they are weighing heavy on him. I then looked to my left seeing that I was laying on his arm.

"Alex, what are you doing?" I ask, sitting up so he can move his arm.

"I have to use the bathroom. You were zonked out." Alex said, rubbing at the back of his neck.

"Did you stay up all night?" I asked curiously. Alex swings his legs over the edge of the bed to sit upright.

"Don't flatter yourself. You fell asleep on my arm and didn't want to disturb you by moving it from under your head. I tried to make myself comfortable but I'm not a back sleeper." Alex answered.

"So, you got some sleep?"

"A little but it was a restless sleep. I couldn't get comfortable." He said, rubbing his eyes. I watch as he makes his way over to the bathroom. I reach over to the nightstand to grab my phone.

I click my phone on to see 8:30 AM is the current time. I know that Alex must be very tired if he had trouble sleeping last night. I sit up leaning against the wall and bring my knees up to my chest. I wrap my arms around them waiting for Alex to emerge from the bathroom. Alex steps out of the bathroom moments later, flicking the lights off to the bathroom.

"Why don't you go take a nap?"

"I'm a man, we don't nap." Alex said.

"Bull crap. You're tired and you need some sleep if you're going to do a match today."

"Well, I would rather go for some coffee and would love to have some company." Alex said.

"I'll keep you company, which is the least I can do. Just let me put a new patch on." I said scooting to the edge of the bed and pulled on my shoes. Alex plops down at the end of the bed, I glance at him, seeing him pulling his shoes back on too.

"You were zonked out last night, you went dead weight on me."

"Sorry, medicines always seem to knock me out and that is why I never take any unless I absolutely need to." I say as my phone begins to ring. I pull it to me seeing my mom's name.

"Who is it?"

"My mom, I'll meet you down there in a moment." I said.

"I'll wait."

"Nah, why don't you go get Chris?"

"Great, I love waking him. Chris isn't a morning person." Alex said, smiling evilly. He heads out of my room, and I quickly pick up the call before it is sent to voicemail.

"Hey mom." I say as I keep an eye on the door to make sure

the coast is clear.

"Hey, how is the cruise?"

"Well, I got seasick but now I'm wearing the patch."

"Have you met anyone?"

"Well...."

"Well?"

"Sort of, but this isn't a singles cruise."

"What type of cruise is it?" My mom asks, I can sense confusion in her voice.

"It's a wrestling cruise."

"You don't watch wrestling though. "

"I know, mom. I'm kind of roped into it now, aren't I?"

"But are you having fun?"

"Yeah, I guess you can say I'm having fun." I said.

"You guess?" My mom asked.

"Fine, I'm having fun. Mom, why did you call?"

"The school sent home some paperwork yesterday. I didn't want to bother you with all the traveling you were doing but the paperwork needs signatures. Am I able to sign it?"

"You should be. What's the paperwork about?"

"Testing for lice and his spine."

"Got it." I knew exactly which testing they were doing. I heard Xavier screaming and running around in the background. He was probably running around with either a dinosaur or Batman. "What is Xavier doing?" I asked curiously.

"He is pretending to make Batman fly." My mom said, chuckling.

"But Batman doesn't fly."

"He doesn't know that. Xavier, your mom is on the phone." My mom said.

"Mommy!" Xavier said as I hear him running and grabbing

the phone, "Hi mommy, how is the big boat?"

"It's fun, it's a little too big for me."

"When can I go on a boat?"

"Next year, I'll bring you on the boat with me." I said.

"What do you do on the boat?"

"We play games, we swim, we dance. We do anything you can think of." I said.

"I want to go! I love to swim and dance."

"I'll take you next year. What did you do last night?"

"Grandma and I camped in my room, we put up a tent and everything. We made s'mores, but we didn't cook our marshmallows since we didn't have a fire. We made popcorn and watched my Dinosaurs tape. Grandma even made me hot chocolate."

"Sounds fun, what are you guys doing today?"

"After school, Grandma is going to take me to the gym with her and then we are going to Chuck E. Cheese."

"Behave and don't run off from grandma."

"I won't, mommy. I miss and love you!" Xavier said.

"I miss and love you too. I'll be home Monday evening."

"Okay, mommy." He says as he hands the phone over to my mom.

"I have to let you go, I need to get ready for work and take Xavier to school."

"Okay, take it easy and please keep an eye on him."

"I will, he is my grand kid."

"I know, but I worry."

"Don't worry too much and have fun."

"I'll try."

"It shouldn't be that hard. Love you."

"Love you too." I say as I hang up the phone. The moment

the call ends, my phone begins ringing again. Chris' name was illuminating on the screen. I swipe my finger to answer the call. "Hey Chris."

"How come Chris has your number and I don't?" Alex asked, I can hear the agitation in his voice.

"Why do you have Chris's phone?"

"Because he's in the bathroom and I like going through people's phones." Alex says and I can tell he is smiling.

"He has my number in case he needs help."

"Nothing else?"

"No, what else would we do?" I asked. My instant thought is that Alex was thinking that Chris and I were dating, yet again. I could never date a client, even though Chris is very handsome and has a great personality. But Chris and I would never work out as a couple.

"I don't know." Alex says when I hear a door open on the other side.

"Why are you on my phone?!" I hear Chris yell on the other side.

"Good-bye Alex." I said hanging up. I head out of my room and down to the main floor. I wait for the two men to come from Chris's room.

"Give me the number!" Alex said loudly, his booming raspy voice caught my attention. I look over my shoulder seeing Alex and Chris walking my way.

"No, you should have gotten it when you had the chance."

"Dude, come on!" Alex begged.

"What are you guys fighting about?" I asked.

"I'm trying to get your phone number from Chris." Alex truthfully answered.

"No, you're not allowed to have my number." I said with a

smile.

"I'll have it by the end of the weekend and that is a guarantee." Alex said determined.

"Ooohhh, we are so scared of you Alex." I said, rolling my eyes. To be honest, I don't think that I would mind if he has my number.

"You should be." Alex said.

"Lord knows I am." Chris says as we approach two steps. I step in front of Chris to make sure he doesn't fall. "Are you feeling better?"

"Yeah, much. And how nice of you to suggest to Alex to buy me pads." I said with a chuckle.

"I didn't know." Chris said with a shrug of his shoulders.

"What'd mom want?" Alex asked.

"She wanted to know how the cruise was going and if I met anyone." I say as Alex pulls open the door letting me walk in before he lets go of the door. The door closes on Chris.

"What the heck man?" Chris yells through the glass door.

"Alex!" I say as I playfully smack Alex.

"What? Just because he has a busted knee doesn't mean he can't open a simple door." Alex said. I sigh before pulling the door open for Chris.

"Thank you, Tara." Chris says smiling before he turns to Alex and sticks his tongue out at him. I help Chris to a table and put his crutches aside so no one will trip over them.

"What do you want?" I ask Chris.

"Um, just black coffee."

"Ew, seriously?" I ask grossed out that he drinks his coffee like that.

"What is wrong with that?"

"I never met anyone that drank it straight up black." I said.

"I do, don't be hating." Chris said, chuckling a tad at the way he said it. I go to join Alex in the short line. Alex looks like he is about to pass out from exhaustion at any moment. Alex stands there with his eyes shut, he is probably trying to catch some moments of shut eye at any chance he can get just to make it through the day.

"I'm sorry about the restless night." I said. I feel guilty that he couldn't sleep last night because of me. Alex opens his eyes, looking over his shoulder at me and a smile creeps onto his face. I wasn't sure if I should be flattered or creeped out.

"Don't worry about it. Do you know that you talk in your sleep?"

"I do not."

"Do too. Want to know what you said?" Alex asked.

"What did I say?"

"You said 'Alex, you're so hot! Oh Alex, you're so muscular.'" Alex tries to say it in a girly voice.

"Shut up, I did not." I said shoving him to get him to shut up.

"Did too."

"I have never talked in my sleep before, why start now?"

"How do you know you never talked in your sleep? You are asleep so you wouldn't know." He pointed out.

"I don't, but no one has ever complained about it before."

"I wasn't complaining." Alex says as he steps up to the counter to order his drink, "I'll have a café Americano."

"What is that?" I asked curiously.

"I'll let you have a sip of it."

"What makes you think I want a sip of it?"

"That is the only way to truly understand what it tastes like."

"I'll think about it." I said as he pays and steps aside to let me order the drinks for Chris and I.

61

"Iced Vanilla Latte? I sure hope that's your drink and not Chris's." Alex says as he is handed his drink.

"It's mine, I think it's a little too girly for Chris."

"I won't put it past Chris, he is more girly than he lets on." Alex says as I chuckle.

"You're so mean to him."

"Am not. That is what brothers do." Alex said. I am handed the two drinks I had ordered and carry them to our table. I hand Chris his cup of plain black coffee that he requested.

"Thanks, how much was it?" Chris asked.

"Don't worry about it. You can bring me coffee when we get back on land." I said.

"Well, that's smart. He can barely walk with his crutches; much less would he be able to carry coffee." Alex said, sipping his coffee.

"I use a wheelchair at the hotel dude." Chris said.

"But still." Alex said with a shrug.

"You're just jealous she asked me to bring her coffee." Chris said.

"Am not." Alex said sternly and nudged Chris to shut up. Alex refuses to make eye contact with me. Maybe he was getting jealous? I don't know why unless he is starting to get feelings too. If he was beginning to get feelings, it would explain why he stayed up last night.

"Do you guys do this all the time?" I asked, looking between the two men.

"Not really. Why? Is it annoying?" Alex asked.

"No. You're the first pair of friends I have met that bicker." I say as I sip my coffee.

"We don't bicker. We just love getting under each other's skin." Chris says as he sips his coffee.

"You know what I was thinking about last night?" Alex asked.

"I'm sure you will tell us anyway." Chris said.

"Tara, what made you think we were strippers? I mean, I understand the posters show all us men in our skimpy trunks, but how does that scream stripper? What kind of strip club name is 'Pure Gold' anyway?"

"Well, you got to remember at the time I was under the impression that this was a singles cruise. When you're on a singles cruise, you wouldn't expect wrestling, would you?" I asked.

"True. But Pure Gold? What did you think Pure Gold meant?" Alex asked.

"Pure Gold? I thought it meant that you would...never mind." I said, feeling my cheeks burning from embarrassment. I couldn't even finish explaining what my mind had thought with that name.

"Tell us." Chris said, trying to lure me into telling them. A creepy smile begins to come across Alex's face like he finally put two and two together of what I had thought.

"Chris, do you really need to ask that?" Alex asked with a laugh.

"Obviously." Chris said. Alex leaned over to whisper into Chris's ear, Chris turned to look at me with big eyes. Alex continues to whisper in his ear. I can't keep eye contact; I look down at my drink and play with the straw in my drink. "Ooohhh! You are one dirty girl. How come we weren't friends before?"

"Because we were professional and in a professional setting, you don't say 'let's talk dirty.'" I said.

"If you did that to me, it would have been instant friendship." Chris said.

"It was kind of hot hearing you say that." Alex said as he took a sip of his coffee, and he wasn't able to make eye contact with me.

"I'm leaving." I said standing up to leave, I didn't want to take this anymore.

"No, don't leave me with him! Alex won't help me." Chris said, grabbing my hand.

"You have my number, but this time don't let him call me." I said nodding towards Alex.

"Why can't I call you?" Alex asked.

"Because you know enough already."

"Do not." Alex retorted.

"Whatever. I want to go brush my teeth; I still have that acidic taste in my mouth. " I said. My mouth still seems very acidic and chalky from being sick last night.

"I'll walk you back, I have to get ready for the Q & A session and wrestling match." Alex said standing up.

"Guys, I need help here." Chris said.

"You got it Chris; you don't need us." Alex said, patting Chris on the shoulder.

"Alex, let's help the man." I say as I grab the crutches and hand them over to Chris. Chris pulls himself up and rests them under his armpits. I pick up the two cups of coffee to carry.

"Chris is just being a baby." Alex said.

"Am not. I can't do everything by myself."

"Can you still go to the bathroom by yourself?" Alex asked.

"Yes, I'm not that handicapped." Chris said. I open the door for Chris and shut it on Alex. Alex stands on the other side of the door giving me a dirty look.

"That was payback for doing it to Chris earlier." I said

making a face at him through the glass door.

"Payback is a horrid thing." Alex said. Alex pushes the door open to walk through while a father and son are walking towards us.

"Dynamite Duo!" The son said pointing to the two men beside me. Both Alex's and Chris's faces light up with joy.

"Hey buddy!" Alex said squatting down to be the same height as the kid. I step aside to watch the interaction between the boy and Alex. I was intrigued to see how Alex would handle kids.

"Hi Alex, may I get a picture and an autograph?" The boy asked.

"Absolutely! You're even wearing our shirt. You're an awesome kid."

"He's a big fan." The father said, gripping at the boy's shoulders. The boy nods his head yes aggressively.

"Why don't I take the photo for you?" I offered.

"You don't mind?" The father asks as Alex looks up at me with a smirk.

"Not at all." I say as the father hands me his phone. I switch positions with him, and Alex picks up the little kid.

"You got to pose, show me your muscles." Alex said. Alex flexes his arm to show off his muscles and has the little boy do it too. I snap the picture and make sure it comes out okay before handing the phone back to the father. Alex sets the boy down. "Will I see you later at our Q & A?"

"Yeah!" The boy said excitedly.

"See you then." Alex said, sticking his hand out to give the kid a high five. The father grabs onto the kid's hand to walk off after the boy gives Alex a high-five. It was nice to see that Alex was good with kids, especially if we end up becoming more than just friends. I would want a guy that is good with kids, so Alex had won some brownie points with that.

"You're good with kids." I said towards Alex.

"Well, I deal with one every day." Alex said, nodding towards Chris.

"I'm not a kid. You're more of a kid than me." Chris said.

"We are all kids at heart." I said as I picked up the two coffee's I had set down to take the picture. I glance at Chris, "You're doing the Q & A too?"

"Yeah, it's going to be fun trying to get into that darn ring." Chris said.

"It isn't that hard." Alex said.

"For you, but if you haven't noticed this cast on my leg." Chris says as he lifts his leg up the best he could to show off his cast.

"Cast be darned, you're getting in that ring." Alex said as he sipped his coffee as we approached the stairs.

"Why do we always take the stairs? There's a ramp right there!" Chris said.

"Walk around then." Alex said. Alex and I wait at the top of the ramp watching Chris hobble his way up the ramp.

"Are you sure you don't want to try and get a wheelchair? It'll be easier." I said.

"No, I'm going to power through this." Chris said.

"Fine." I said, rolling my eyes while sipping my coffee.

"He's the most stubborn." Alex said.

"He's just strong willed." I said.

"It's part of our egos. We are supposed to be these strong muscle men that are able to take care of themselves, not afraid of anything. We are like superheroes to these kids but when we get hurt, we need help from others to do normal day things."

"Not all injuries are that bad. Having broken ribs you don't need as much help as a broken limb." I stated.

"Yeah, but it does hit our egos having to ask for help." Alex said.

"The best was when AJ broke his arm, and he couldn't button his pants. We had to take turns going to the bathroom with him to help undo and redo his pants." Chris said.

"That is what friends are for." I said.

"Have you broken anything?" Alex asked.

"When I was six, I chipped one of my front teeth. I broke my wrist in three spots at once." I said not wanting to bring up the leg Xavier broke.

"You're an overachiever." Chris said.

"I try my best." I say as we approach his room, "You need help?" I asked as he stopped and moved his one crutch to pull out his key.

"I got this part at least." He said as he unlocked the door. I open the door and hold it open for him so he can hobble in. I set our coffee aside to help him sit down. I move his crutches somewhere where he can easily grab them if he needs to move about.

"We'll be back to get you for the Q & A." I say as I pick up my coffee.

"Alright, I will try to be ready by the time it begins. When is it?" Chris asked Alex.

"Ours is at two, you have a few hours." Alex said.

"Enough time for me to at least take a shower." Chris said.

"If you can't take a shower in four hours, I'll be worried." Alex said.

"Come on Alex, let him do his thing." I said pushing Alex towards the door to give Chris some privacy and alone time.

Chapter Seven:

Alex and I walk out of Chris's room, I pull the door closed until I hear the soft click meaning it is fully shut. It is now just Alex and I, alone.

"So, he gets your number, and I don't?" Alex asked with a perk brow.

"He's a special case. I don't see you with a broken leg."

"I'll try to break my leg in my match today." Alex teased.

"Please don't." I said as I sipped my coffee.

"You will stay for my match, won't you?"

"Isn't it right after your Q & A?"

"Yeah."

"Wouldn't it be rude of me to leave then?" I asked, staring ahead of me not wanting to make eye contact with him.

"Yeah, it'll be rude. I don't see you being a rude person."

"I can be rude, but I choose not to. I have to be a role model."

"Role model for who?" Alex asked curiously.

Oh crap, I forgot he doesn't know about Xavier yet. I think to myself and am mentally smacking myself on the forehead.

"I meant that I have to set an example for my employees at work since I am the boss and everything." I lie, but it isn't a full lie. I am the manager so I do have to be a good example for them.

"Oh." Alex says as the elevator doors open, and he lets me climb on the elevator first. He steps on, pushing the proper button as I mentally wipe my brow knowing that it was a close one. "So, you're a manager?"

"To an extent. I still have upper management I need to report to." I said.

"Of what?"

"Of services."

"What type of services?" Alex asks when the doors open yet again, and he lets me climb off first with him directly on my heel. I step aside so he can walk beside me down the open corridor to our rooms.

"Medical services, not those types of services Alex." I said.

"I wasn't thinking about that, you're a big pervert. I can see where your mind is this weekend." Alex said with a chuckle. He smiles and runs a hand through his hair before he takes a sip of his coffee.

"Honestly, did you get any sleep last night?"

"No, I didn't. I was worried, I couldn't calm my worries down enough to sleep." Alex explained with a glance over at me.

"You seriously don't like sick people?"

"Seriously." Alex said.

"Thanks. No one has ever taken care of me before besides my mom when I was younger. I can never afford to be sick; I need all the work I can get. "

"So you're the type of person that never misses a day of work.

You're there even if you don't need to be. How many days of work have you missed since you were hired?" Alex asked.

"One, but that is not counting the days I took off for this. I'm still sort of working if you count me helping Chris." I say as I sip my coffee when we approach my room.

"So, how many days is that? Four to five days? Why don't you take more time off?"

"I can't, okay?" I say as I unlock my door. I practically dove into my room, and slam the door in his face.

I feel tears in my eyes, I don't want to explain to him why I work so much. I close the connecting door and lock it before he can get to it. I want to be alone. I put my coffee down so I can climb onto my bed, I open the small window to get some cool air into the room.

I bring my knees to my chest, I need to talk to someone. Mom? No, she's busy with work or Xavier. Stephanie? Well, she is sick, so she'll be home. I push her name in my contact list. Listening to it ring, waiting for the click. I never date because I'm afraid that I'll be judged, or the guy won't understand if I tell them the truth. Dave broke the engagement off because he didn't want kids, didn't want Xavier, and made me feel that no man will love me the same.

I'm afraid of finding someone that I am truly attracted to, love and someone that is good with kids but will hurt my feelings after finding out about Xavier yet again. Why don't men ever want to date a girl with kids? I think to myself when I hear the phone click, and that means Stephanie had picked up.

"Hey Tara, how is the cruise going?" Stephanie asks in a weak voice.

"It's going good." I said. I honestly don't know why I felt so upset with the conversation with Alex.

Chapter Seven:

"Bull crap. You wouldn't be calling me if it was going well."

"Ok, there is a guy."

"OoohhH!"

"Shut up, Stephanie." I say when I hear a knock at the connecting door.

"Tara, can we talk? I'm sorry if I made you upset." Alex asked.

"Is that him?" Stephanie asked, I look at the connecting door that he must be standing on the other side of.

"Yes."

"What'd he do?"

"He asked me why I didn't take more time off."

"Tara!" She yells at me, "Honestly girl, it was a simple freaking question. You didn't have to flip out on him. You could have shrugged or said you had no reason to take time off."

"But I'm afraid of how he will react with Xavier."

"You don't have to tell him about Xavier."

Another knock at the door, "Tara, I'm sorry. I would still love for you to come to the match today. Chris may need some help."

"He sounds very handsome. You need to work it girl."

"He is very handsome. Oh god, what am I saying?!" I said smacking myself on the forehead.

"You should be saying, 'Thank you Stephanie!' What does he look like?"

"You know Stephanie, you didn't help me at all. I should be ignoring you; this isn't a singles cruise by the way."

"It's not? My bad." Stephanie said with laughter, "I need details."

"Good-bye, Stephanie." I said hanging up on her.

I set my phone aside and I know Stephanie means well.

71

Stephanie did have a point, I didn't have to say anything about needing the money for Xavier or bills. I could have just said I had no reason to miss work. I got upset over nothing. All Alex asked was why I didn't take more days off and nothing about that is bad.

Why do I always do this? I always overreact and get sensitive about everything people say? Alex was just trying to get to know me better. I think I just try to find reasons to end relationships before they even start. I think it is self-destruction. I feel that Dave calling the engagement off left me not only heartbroken but worrisome about any potential love interest. I deeply loved him, I thought he felt the same. For him to call off the wedding, showed his true feelings for me. Maybe I wasn't made out to be loved. I feared rejection again. I am still so fragile.

Maybe I care more about Alex because he's friends with Chris. I have built a friendship with Chris over the last few weeks and will continue seeing him post-cruise. No, I shouldn't care what Chris thinks since he's only a customer. After his leg heals, hasta la vista baby. Alex is just my neighbor for the weekend and we both just want to have a good time.

Alex probably has a girlfriend and he's here to work, not to try to make a love connection. I was getting angrier with myself the more I got to thinking. I lean my head back against the wall looking out the window, drowning myself in self-pity when a knock came to the door again.

"Tara, I'm sorry for whatever I said. I don't know what I had said that was so bad, but I would love for you to come with me. If you would only open this door." Alex said. I look at my phone seeing that it is only noon and am curious why he is leaving early. I realize he and Chris will probably go grab some lunch.

A few moments passed, I began to think he left, but Alex continued "I guess you're not opening the door. I hope you have a change of heart; I would still love for you to be out there." Alex said through the door. I felt guilty, I promised him I would go, and I was breaking the promise. Regardless of how I felt, I should still go for him. I jump off the bed, bolt to the door as quickly as I can but I don't make it in time. Alex was already gone.

Crap! I thought to myself. I go over to where I had hung my clothes to try to find a new outfit but realize all I had packed were clothes that I considered risqué for me.

I grab the knee length black skirt with a purple spaghetti strap. I pull down the jean jacket to top off the ensemble. I hurriedly take a shower in hopes not to miss too much of his Q & A or match. I brush my teeth and blow dry my hair just enough to be able to style it.

I walk out of the bathroom to slide on a pair of tennis shoes. Out of the corner of my eye, I noticed Gary, Xavier's toy dinosaur, sticking out of my suitcase. Xavier must have dropped it in my bag by accident, I guess he was going on an adventure with me.

"Oh, Xavier." I say as I pull the toy out of my bag and hold it in my hands. I couldn't help the smile that crept onto my face. "Do this for Xavier. Alex is great with kids, and I think Xavier will love Alex."

I grab my purse before heading out of the room. I check my phone seeing that it is now 1300, and I want to take my time to get there. I am taking deep breaths trying to think of ways to explain my freak out to Alex. I mean if he is anything like Chris, he will understand.

I take the long way around to not take any chances of running into them. When I find the wrestling ring, Alex is helping Chris into the ring already. I check the time on my phone, it is 1330 so it is earlier than planned. I lean against a pillar, trying to stay in the shadows as I watch the two men being handed a microphone. I can tell Alex is scanning the crowd, he is probably looking for me.

Chapter Eight:

I took a step back to be further in the shadows from the floor above. I did not want Alex to be able to see me quite yet. I want him to know so he knows I didn't break my promise but I was quite nervous after my freak out. Alex's body language is completely different than before. Maybe he is out of it? A bit sad or a bit angry? Maybe his mind is clouded by what happened? Either way, it is all my fault. I am still too nervous to step out of the shadows to let him know I am here, I'm hoping as time passes, I'll get the courage to show myself.

"Hey, guys. Chris, what's going on with your leg?" The MC asked.

"My knee is still recovering. The doctors put the cast on after surgery so I won't mess up the stitching or anything like that. I should be back by the end of March. I'm hoping for sooner though." Chris answered. His time frame of recovery sounds about right with the amount of physical therapy he was going to need.

"Me too. I miss my buddy." Alex said, patting Chris on the

shoulder.

"Alex, with your tag partner out of action, has things changed?" The MC asked.

"Obviously. I can't take part in any tag team matches as of late. There is no one better to tag with than Chris here. I hope that I can keep myself busy doing solo matches until he can return to the ring." Alex answered.

"Alright, are you two ready for some fan questions?" The MC asked.

"Bring it on." Chris said. I see both men scanning the crowd, Chris's sight seems to be fixated in my general direction. I bite at my bottom lip, unsure if he can make me out or not. I thought I was tucked enough into the shadows that you couldn't tell too much of my features.

"'How do you prepare yourself for matches?' Tommy asked." The MC read off an index card.

"Well, we stretch and warm-up before any match because you need to be on top of your game physically. We then recite the National Anthem to try to put our minds at ease. You need to have a clear mind walking into this ring." Alex answered.

"If you aren't focused on what is taking place in the ring it puts the risk of injuries higher. While you're wrestling, all you should be thinking about is the match. If you're not, then you can wrongfully do something causing injuries to yourself or your opponent." Chris stated.

"Mental state in the match is just as important as your physical state."

"'Are you guys single?' Margaret asks." The MC read. I need to thank this Margaret lady; I was interested to know if Alex was single or not.

"Currently, yes." Chris answered, I think that was the first time I had ever seen Chris blush.

"Dude, why are you blushing?" Alex asked, nudging Chris.

"Shut up and answer the question." Chris said, nudging Alex back.

"Yes, I'm single. But I'm currently interested in someone." Alex said. He was interested in someone? I had no chance then. I can't compete with this other lady. A feeling of defeat came over me that he liked someone else.

"Who is the lucky person?" The MC asked.

"I prefer not to answer" Alex said.

"Same person asks, would you want kids?" The MC asked, great question. I was anticipating the answer. Alex's answer would determine if this would even work out between us. If Alex didn't want kids, then having Xavier would be a deal breaker. I was praying that he would say yes to give me some glimmer of hope.

"I would love kids of my own someday. I want one boy and one girl but would totally do adoption or foster care as well if the girl would be interested. I love kids." Alex answered. A big sigh of relief overcame me to hear that answer and I couldn't help but to be giddy. I felt the courage to slowly step forward towards the edge of the crowd to show that I was here.

"That's because you're a giant kid yourself." Chris said.

"That I am. I'm a giant kid myself, so I tend to love kids." Alex said.

"What about you, Chris? How do you feel about kids?"

"I love them, I would love to have kids of my own one day." Chris answered.

"Okay. Who is the one wrestler, past or present, you would love to wrestle?"

"I would have to say Bret Hart." Chris said.

"Good choice, Alex?" The MC said.

"I would have to go with Andre the Giant." Alex said.

"He will kick your butt." Chris said with a laugh.

"I don't care, he's a giant and giants are awesome." Alex said.

"Here is a good one. Out of all the big and famous tag-teams, which one tag-team past or present do you think you two are most like?" The MC asked.

"I personally think we base a lot of our stuff off of the Rockers." Chris said.

"But not as bright, we don't dig the bright colors as if you couldn't tell."

"And we're more rocker." Chris said, chuckling. Another song began to play through the sound system, which I wasn't sure what it meant. I saw two other guys emerge from the makeshift changing room. Alex and the MC began to help Chris through the ropes to get him out of the ring. My heart beating faster in worry that he was going to get hurt but leave it to Chris to know what would give me a heart attack. When Chris got to his feet, our eyes meet, and a smile comes across his face. Chris KNEW I was here.

Chris hobbles over to the security guard, seeing him talking with the guard. Chris points at me, and the guard follows his point right to me. *What were they talking about?* I thought to myself. I watch the guard walk through the curtain area and beeline to me.

"Chris has requested you to come sit beside him." The guy said.

"Did he say why?" I asked.

"He said you were his assistant for the weekend." The guy said.

"Fine, whatever." I said with a roll of my eye. I was upset

78

that Chris had pulled strings to get me special treatment. I was escorted through the curtain area trying not to trip over the cords for the camera crew and the thick black mat. The security guard escorted me to where Chris was sitting. "What the heck was that?" I asked as I walk around the guard and caught myself flinching with every loud bang of the ring.

"You're my assistant, sit. If you see me duck, you duck, if you see me lift my feet, lift your feet." Chris said as I sat down nodding my head. "Are you hiding anything from me?"

"Chris, the only thing I've ever hid was Xavier. You figured that secret out the second time you met me. Don't tell Alex, please?" I asked in a beg. It isn't that I don't want Alex to know about Xavier, but I am afraid of how Alex is going to take it. And if Alex is going to find out, it has to be from me and not from Chris.

Chris claims that having a child won't scare all men off, but I don't know Alex well enough to know if he will or won't. I didn't want to ruin what Alex and I have, if we have anything, by telling him that I am a mom.

I wasn't sure what I feel towards Alex, but I find myself liking him. I don't know if it is because he is the first guy I had started to feel this way about since my ex or that Alex is the first guy that seemed to show interest in me in years.

"Are you an alien?" Chris asked, bringing me out of my thoughts.

"No, I'm not an alien." I said laughing.

"You aren't male, are you?"

"No, wait…" I paused, beginning to grope myself to make sure I had all the female parts, "No, I'm not a male."

"Are you a zombie or a vampire?" Chris asked.

"No."

"Have you ever had sexual feelings towards a horse?"

"What the heck is up with these questions?" I asked confused but couldn't help but to laugh at the questions he was asking.

"I realized I don't know the real you. I just know the girl that works hard and pushes me in a wheelchair." Chris said.

"Chris, I'm a thirty something female that works for a living. I have a college degree at the University of Las Vegas in hospitality. I have one sister, a mother, and a father that abandoned my family when I was four. I was not hatched by an egg, I didn't fly to earth on a spaceship, nor have I had any sexual relations with any animals in my lifetime."

"Okay, but have you ever had an out of body experience?"

"I wish I was having one right now." I said.

"Okay."

"What's with all these weird questions?" I asked curiously.

"Because," Chris had begun to answer when Alex was thrown out of the ring. He landed on the mat before he rolled onto his back and laid at our feet.

"Alex." I said with a smile.

"Tara?" Alex asked. His face lit up with happiness and a smile crept across his lips.

"Dude, match!" Chris said, pointing to the ring.

"Right." Alex said with a nod. I let out a chuckle at Alex as he got to his feet to get back into the ring to finish the match.

"Because why?" I asked. I turn my attention back to Chris and try to strike the conversation back up. I want to get to the bottom of why Chris is interrogating me.

"It's nothing." He said, shaking his head with a laugh.

"It's obviously something."

"It's nothing, trust me." Chris said smiling. I jump and scream a couple times when suplexes or slams are performed.

"They're okay. You know that, right?"

"I know, Alex explained that you are trained on how to take the hits."

"It doesn't hurt that bad." Chris said.

"How does that not hurt?" I asked when Alex got body slammed into the mat.

"It's going to sound weird but the harder you throw yourself down the less it hurts but the less you throw yourself the more it hurts."

"That doesn't make any sense."

"That's how it is." Chris said as he stretched his arm out to rest on the back of my chair.

"Weird. What is the ring made of?"

"Well, the frame is steel. There is wood that fills in the empty space in the frame then an inch or so of padding then the mat. The poles are steel obviously, the ropes are steel cables wrapped multiple times with certain colored duct tape and where they meet on the steel cable is covered with a padded turnbuckle." Chris explained.

"How can you sit here and tell me that it doesn't hurt?" I asked.

"It doesn't, if you do it right."

"Is that why you have to be trained for months or years?" I asked.

"Yep, like any sport you need to practice and learn everything. Wrestling is more complicated than other sports and it takes a whole lot longer to learn. You don't only need to learn the physical aspect of it, but you need to learn the mentality behind it."

"It sounds hard." I said.

"It isn't the hardest job." Chris said.

"Yeah, it doesn't seem hard coming from the one that has a messed-up knee." I joked.

"Hey! Injuries happen."

"Like how life happens?" I asked.

"Yeah, you have to live life in the fast lane and take risks, even if it results in injuries. It's just a step-back." Chris said.

"I'm not that risky...I don't take risks because I'm scared of the smallest things." I said.

"Is that your biggest secret? It's that you're scared of everything?"

"There are a lot of things that I keep secret, we all have secrets we don't tell people. You ended up finding mine out." I said.

"Alex has a lot of secrets. I know his secrets too." Chris said.

"Alex isn't a part of this conversation." I said. I am kind of uncomfortable talking about Alex because I didn't know how I felt towards him or how he felt towards me.

"Oh, he is."

"How so?" I asked Chris. I turn to look at him instead of watching the match we are supposed to be watching, and of course that is the moment Alex got the pin.

"Nothing." Chris said as I look back to the ring seeing Alex's arm being raised in victory. I stand up grabbing the crutches that security had put aside, bringing them to Chris and helping him to his feet.

I stand there helping put the crutches under Chris's arms when I feel an arm wrap around my neck. I look at the hand that was resting on my left shoulder before I look to my right to see Alex. He has a smile plastered on his face. His face is just glowing with happiness.

"You came!" Alex said happily as he pulls me into a hug. I didn't know what to do. I slowly wrap my arms around him to embrace the hug.

"I promised I would, I never break a promise." I said after he let me go but continued resting his arm on my shoulder.

"Never?" Alex asked.

"Not yet." I said.

"Challenge accepted." Alex said as Chris rolled his eyes. We let him walk in front of us around the ring and Alex keeps his arm wrapped around my shoulders. It would have felt rude to push it off, plus I didn't mind.

When I walk behind the curtain with them, there was a huge mess, but what else can you expect? They are men after all. They don't have much time before their matches to make sure everything is put away neatly. I step out from Alex's embrace and help Chris sit down. I hold onto his crutches; I try putting them under my arms. Surprisingly, I am able to and am swinging myself on them.

"Well, we found a way to keep her entertained." Alex said smiling. I look over when I see him noticing me.

"Sorry." I say as I slide off the crutches, embarrassed that I had got caught. The curtain is flung open, and the other tag team walked through the open curtain.

"Good match." The one that was in the match said.

"Same to you." Alex said, smacking his hand before fist bumping it.

"Who are you?" The other said.

"Oh, I'm Tara." I said sticking my hand out to shake theirs.

"Are you allowed back here?" The first guy asked.

"Yeah, she's cool. She's my assistant." Chris explained.

"I am NOT your assistant." I say with an attitude and plant my hands on my hips.

"Yeah, you kind of are." Chris said with a laugh.

"You're not paying me." I said.

"Dang, she has an attitude." The first guy said.

"It's not an attitude, it's just her." Chris says as I gasp in shock that he just said that.

"I just don't like being called something I'm not. I'm a friend." I say as I stick my hand out to shake theirs again in hopes they will shake my hand this time around.

"Nice to meet you, I'm Jim." The first guy said, shaking my hand finally, "This is Rob." Jim said, pointing to his tag partner.

"In wrestling terms, they are Dollar Billz." Alex explains before he turns to look at Rob and Jim, "She doesn't watch wrestling."

"Alex." I said smacking him.

"What? It's true." Alex said.

"If you don't watch wrestling, how does a pretty girl like you end up on a wrestling cruise?" Jim asks as he sits down and begins undoing his boots.

"It's a long story which will end with me killing my friend and Alex is close to second on that list." I said.

"All that matters is that you're here now, sweetie." Rob jumped in.

"Yeah, that is all that matters." I say when Chris is finished switching his shoe and I help him to his feet. "I'll walk him back to his room. It was nice meeting you Jim, Rob."

"Pleasure was ours." Jim said with a wink.

"Are all wrestlers flirts?" I asked Chris.

"Nah, just those two and Alex." Chris said as I opened the curtains for him to walk through. I step out behind him to let the curtains fall back to being closed.

Chapter Nine:

I walk out of the curtain behind Chris to walk him back to his room. I want to allow Alex time to finish what he needed to do. Plus, with Chris being on crutches he moves a lot slower so it gives us a head start.

"After seeing your first wrestling match in person, what do you think?" Chris asked.

"It was good. A sport I could get used to watching." I shrugged.

"Why are you shrugging? You always shrug when you don't know."

"How do you know me so well?"

"We have spent too much time together." Chris said smiling.

"Just don't share that information with Alex, he seems to be the kind of guy that will get a kick out of it." I said.

"Kick out of what?" Alex asks as he runs up behind us and steps between us.

"Nothing." I said.

"Know some of the information that I know about her."

Chris said with a wide smile.

"What type of information is that?" Alex asked, smiling as he looks from me to Chris.

"Chris, I will bust your other knee." I threatened.

"You won't bust my knee." Chris said.

"Miss goody two shoes." Alex said as he chuckled.

"Am not, I have a bad side." I say as Chris almost loses his balance as he is trying to pull himself up the stairs. "Whoa there…" I say catching him before he falls back all the way pushing him up further to stand straight on the step.

"Thanks." Chris said.

"Dude, you almost fell!" Alex says as he points and laughs from the top step.

"Shut up!" Chris says as I help him up the rest of the steps.

"Do you have a bad side?" Alex asked.

"I can." I said.

"What is the worst thing you have ever done?" Alex asked, crossing his arms over his chest.

"I stole a piece of candy from a store when I was a kid."

"Seriously? That's it?" Chris asked, stopping, and looking at me with a look of intrigue.

"Yeah, that's my bad side."

"Psh, that isn't that bad." Alex said.

"What is the worst thing you've done?" I asked, crossing my arms over my chest now.

"We vandalized a club once." Chris said laughing.

"Vandalized? How?" I asked in a worried tone. How much do I truly know about these two men? Were they the right crowd for me? Or to bring around Xavier?

"We got in a fist fight with this pair of guys that were harassing these girls. We ended up throwing one through

86

the window and the other guy went through a table." Alex explained as he put his hands in his jacket pockets.

"Those guys were jerks." Chris said, shaking his head in disbelief.

"You guys did it to protect those girls." I said smiling a tad that they only did it out of protecting two girls from two jerks. A sigh of relief came over me, maybe I had misjudged Alex's rough rock star type exterior.

"We got arrested and stayed in jail for one night. The charges were dropped when the girls came forward. We replaced the table and the window at the bar." Alex said.

"And now we get free beers for life." Chris added.

"I bet that's worth it, huh?" I said with a smile.

"Especially after hard days at work." Chris said.

"You're not supposed to be drinking with your medications." I said in my motherly tone and put my hand on my hip, stopping where I was.

"Yes, mother. I haven't drunk a beer since I started taking my medications. Plus, I'm almost done with them anyway." Chris said.

"Good. When was the last time you took your medicine?" I asked, reminding me of such things.

"She is good at her job." Alex said as we turned down a walkway to go to Chris's room.

"Isn't she?" Chris said.

"A lot better than you guys." I joked.

"Ouch!" Alex said, putting his hand over his heart pretending that it hurt, "That really hurt. I may shed a tear."

"As you should." I say as we stop in front of Chris's room.

"He will literally cry." Chris said.

"Do you cry often?" I asked Alex.

"Real men cry." Alex said.

"Like real men wear pink?" I asked. Chris unlocked the door and I push it open for him. I step into the room, hold the door open for Chris so he can hobble into the room.

"Real men do wear pink and have a good cry. I never had a full out cry fest." Alex said, trying to explain himself. I let go of the door before he stepped through, "Hey, I'm walking here!" Alex exclaimed, catching the door before it hit him.

"I forgot about you."

"You're just aiming to make me cry now, aren't you?" Alex asked.

"It's not working if you're smiling."

"Is she really this hardcore?" Alex asks, pointing to me with his thumb looking at Chris. I walk over to Chris helping him scoot up his bed and slide a pillow under his knee.

"She can be." Chris said.

"Hey." I said smacking Chris playfully.

"She isn't mean of sorts; she just loves joking around." Chris said, I begin to fix things on his bed.

"You want to change out of your ring gear?" I asked, noticing the shorts that were similar to Alex's.

"I can do that on my own." Chris said.

"We all know where her mind is this weekend. First she thinks we are strippers and now she wants to help you out of your clothes." Alex said snickering a tad. I grab a pillow and throw it at him. Alex catches the pillow before he is hit with it.

"Dang, good reflexes." I was impressed by the catch.

"He's a wrestler, he's supposed to have good reflexes. If not, he wouldn't be a good wrestler." Chris said.

"Is that a compliment Chris?" Alex asked.

"Duh! We are the best tag-team around." Chris said.

"Yeah, you guys are the best." I said, rolling my eyes.

"Yes, we are." Alex said.

"Well, if you need anything you know my number. I'm going to go get something to eat before I explore the rest of the boat." I said.

"Yep, I'll call you if I need anything." Chris said, smirking. I turn around seeing Alex standing at the end of Chris' bed. I walk past him and out of the room to find the food court. I grab some food to eat, and I eat it at a table by myself.

Afterwards, I walk around the ship taking pictures of the posters and approach the railings that are on the edge of the deck. Standing there you have the perfect view of the ocean blue, I lean against the railing just enjoying the precious view and letting the breeze blow through my hair.

"There you are." I hear the familiar male voice say. I turn around seeing Alex approaching me. I can't help the smile that crosses onto my face.

"Hey." I said looking back at the ocean.

"Is this really wise for a girl that gets seasick?" Alex asked. He steps beside me, and leans against the railing.

"Not really. Oddly, wearing the patch and looking at the ocean doesn't make me feel seasick." I said.

"Thank god you're not feeling sick anymore. I was heading to the meet and greet with all the guys. Do you want to come?" Alex asked.

"Chris going?"

"Does Chris have to go for you to work?" Alex asked in a somewhat offensive tone.

"No, but I was wondering if he needed help." I said truthfully.

"Nah, Chris is already there. Security escorted him to our table." Alex said.

"How does this meet and greet go?" I asked. We both stand up straight and turn around, I let him begin to lead the way.

"You walk around meeting all the wrestlers that you would want to meet, like myself." Alex said smiling.

"I've already met you." I respond.

"Touché, but you can take a picture with me without me having to say no."

"Why would I want a picture with you?" I joke.

"I don't know, to show mom."

"I'll think about it." I say, smirking as he walks beside me.

"Have I told you that you look beautiful tonight?" Alex asked.

"No, but thank you." I said pushing a strand of hair behind my ear.

"No problem." Alex said with a wink.

"How often do you guys do these cruises?" I asked curiously.

"This was our first cruise ever, does that make you feel more special?" Alex asked.

"How is it supposed to make me feel special?"

"To be a part of this…" Alex trailed off as he pulled the doors open to the banquet room that had multiple long tables around the room. Multiple wrestlers sitting on the opposing side of them, and fans were surrounding the middle of the room, "phenomenon." Alex continued.

"You guys truly have a lot of fans." I glance over to him as we step into the room.

"This isn't even half of it." Alex whispered with another wink. He left me at the door to head towards the table Chris was already sitting at. Chris is signing items and taking pictures with fans. There is a sign behind him that reads their tag team name.

I watch Alex walk to his table, he claims the empty seat

next to Chris. I step forward into the madness of fans, I was overwhelmed with the amount of chaos in that room. I walk around the room at first, reading all the different names and tried to remember the faces with the names. I jump in line for the tag team Dollar Billz. They were placed on the opposing side of the room as Alex and Chris. As I got to the front of the line, I stuck my hand out to shake their hands again.

"Hi." I said, nervously pushing a strand of hair behind my ear. Why was I now nervous to meet them but didn't have a care earlier?

"Hey there, sweetie. You decided to come see us instead of those fools?" Jim said with a chuckle. He looks down at an 8 x 10 photo of both of them and signed his autograph with a silver sharpie.

"Yeah, I spend enough time with them. I figure they will be last on my list to meet." I said.

"People can only take so much of them." Rob said.

"May I get a photo?" I asked in hopes they would say yes.

"Absolutely, honey." Jim said. They both stand up, press their cheeks against mine. I stick my phone out to do a selfie with them.

"Thank you so much." I said smiling. I lower my arm after I capture the selfie. "And good match earlier."

"Thanks. Will we see you again?" Jim asked.

"Yeah, considering I'm apparently Chris's assistant." I sighed.

"Don't take any of their crap." Rob said as I grab the photo they signed. I walk around the room making sure Alex and Chris are the last two people I would meet. I am happy with the people I have met thus far, they all seemed nice and down to earth.

I am standing in line to meet Alex and Chris. I am looking

through the pictures on my phone. When it's my turn, Alex's face lights up with a smile.

"Finally decided to come see us?" Alex jokes.

"I guess we aren't that important to her. I thought you loved us." Chris said with a snicker.

"I wanted others to meet you before I got my chance." I say as Alex grabs their photo to sign.

"Sure. We know the real reason." Alex said, rolling his eyes.

"You think you do." I said.

"I do know. I'm smarter than you think." Alex said.

"No, he's not." Chris said shaking his head no. Alex slides the photo over to Chris so he can sign it as well.

"Am too." Alex said offensively.

"I think you're smart to an extent." I said chuckling.

"You want a picture?" Alex asks willingly before I can say anything.

"Um…sure." I said unsure if I wanted to. Alex stands up to pose for the picture and I turn around. Alex presses his cheek against mine as I put my phone out to do a selfie with him.

"Guys, I can't stand up here." Chris said offensively.

"Hold your horses, Chris." Alex turns to look at him right when I snap the photo.

"Way to ruin that photo." I laugh. I flip over to my photos app to show them the photo I had just snapped. Alex and Chris see the picture that Alex ruined, getting them both to laugh too.

"Another one." Alex wraps his arm around me to hold me tight to his embrace. He presses his cheek against mine, smiling wide and I smile just as wide. When we look at the new photo, Chris had photo bombed us by placing himself behind Alex. He had a pout on his face with his arms crossed over his chest, he MADE the picture.

"You made that picture." I said, showing Chris and he chuckled.

"Good." Chris said proudly. I squat down in front of the table, and he leans forward to where our faces are mere inches apart and take a selfie. This time Alex photo bombed us by sitting in the back flicking the camera off.

"Alex!" I said as I see it and he just laughs.

"You're a jerk." Chris said, smacking him.

"Is there any way I can get one of all three of us?" I asked.

"Later." Alex said, winking.

"Kinky." Chris said, he makes a disgusted face when Alex winked.

"You know it." Alex said.

"Wow. I'm going to leave now." I said, grabbing the signed photo.

"Don't leave, just pull up a chair. I need help getting back to my room." Chris said.

"What happened to your guard?" I asked curiously.

"He's a little under the weather." He nods to the guard that now has his head shoved into the garbage can.

"Yeah, I don't need to see that." I said quickly, turning away.

"You're one of those people that gets sick seeing someone else do it." Alex said.

"Yes, I do." I said holding my stomach.

"Please don't." Chris said grossed out.

"Got ya!" I said laughing at their reactions.

"That's something Alex would do." Chris said.

"You're the type of guy that splashes water on someone and pretends to sneeze?" I asked Alex. I step aside to let other fans come up.

"Yeah, it's fun entertainment." Alex said.

"Go grab a chair and pull it up." Chris said, nodding to a stack of chairs.

"Will I get in trouble?"

"You scared?" Alex looked up at me from the picture he was signing.

"No." I said sheepishly.

"Liar." Alex said as Chris signed the picture.

"Watch this." I said leaving the table and going to the stack of chairs. I pull one off the top without getting into any trouble. I carry the chair to the table they were at.

"Good girl." Alex said, clapping a tad in an arrogant type of way. I sit down crossing my legs when I pull out my phone that is vibrating. I see that my mom is calling, I ignore the call and put the phone aside.

"Who did you ignore?" Chris asked.

"My mom." I said.

"OoohhH, you're going to get in trouble for ignoring her." Chris said.

"Am not."

"I would be." Alex said.

"Mama's boy?" I asked.

"No."

"Yes." Chris said as Alex shoved him. They continue posing for pictures and signing autographs until fans begin to leave the room. With no one left in line, Alex caps off his sharpie and finally relaxes in his chair.

"Were you a daddy's girl?" Alex asked.

"Nah, that was my sister."

"You were a mommy's girl?" Chris asked.

"I was neither. Well, when I was younger until about the age

94

ten, I was my mom's girl." I said.

"You were a rebel?" Alex asked.

"Not really." I said as I texted my mom explaining I was out mingling.

"It's that dang puberty, which gets to everyone." Alex said.

"I hate puberty." Chris said.

"I wouldn't say that." I giggle about the way he said it.

"It was the worst time of my life, but now I love the fact I went through puberty." Chris said smiling.

"Why are we having this conversation?" I asked, rolling my eyes.

"Chris started it." Alex said.

"I was just stating the obvious, after puberty it gets a lot better." Chris said.

"Puberty was awkward but I don't want to discuss it further." I said.

"Me neither." Alex said.

"What? I'm not a pervert you guys." Chris said.

"Anyways, I just didn't do the things that my mom liked. Either my mom enjoyed what I did, or my mom didn't like it." I said.

"Isn't that how it always is?" Chris asked as the room had finally been completely emptied except the wrestlers.

"Parents are strange. I vow to support my kids in whatever way even if I dislike it." Alex said. I smirk a tad hearing that and that is the way I want to raise Xavier.

"You say that. I think everyone says that they will raise their kids one way, but they don't." Chris said.

"Not really." I said not thinking before I had spoken.

"You have experience raising a kid?" Alex asked, arching an eyebrow. My body begins to feel all tingly, the room feels like it is closing in on me and my palms become sweaty. Panic. He is going to know. I look at Chris with bugged out eyes then back to Alex.

"Oh, well no. My sister has a kid, and she has stuck to what she had vowed to do." I lie as I stand up quickly wanting to end this conversation before I spill the beans. I drag my chair across the room and stack it back on top of the other chairs. I was hoping that by the time I return the conversation about having kids or being parents had ended.

Chapter Ten:

Before I return to the table, I see Alex standing and stretching his body out. Chris is trying to stand up but is having trouble.

"Alex, you're not going to help him?" I ask as I step in front of Chris. I stick my hands out for him to use to help pull himself up.

"Sorry." Alex says as he watches me help Chris to his feet. Chris tries not to put too much weight on his cast.

"Where are your crutches?" I ask, looking around the area trying to spot them. They were nowhere in sight.

"About that." Chris said, my head snapping up to give him an evil glare and my hand flings to rest on my hip.

"What?" I asked.

"I didn't bring them." Chris said, his face contorted to a cringe. He knew I was going to be angry.

"Why didn't you bring them?" I asked in a stern tone that I would use on Xavier.

"Mother, I was carried." Chris said in a mocking tone and batted his eyelids.

"By who?" I asked. Alex, maybe? I look at Alex, he did have muscles, but had a slimmer body frame. I would be kind of shocked that he would be able to carry Chris along with that cast of his.

"Not me, I'm not that strong." Alex said, holding his hands up.

"My guard." Chris said, nodding to the guard that was green to the face.

"You think we can carry him?" Alex asked.

"Seriously?" I asked.

"Why not? I can lift Chris' weight alone on weight machines, but you'll be there to help."

"Well, this will be fun." Chris said sarcastically.

"It's not a bucket of roses for me either, sweet cheeks." Alex said. Chris wraps his arms around Alex's neck and Alex picks Chris up into a fireman's carry.

"I have to get a picture of this." I said snapping a picture with a laugh.

"That will come back and haunt us." Alex said. I move the table so Alex can walk straight instead of going around it. I try to help as much as I can by holding the doors and stuff for them until we get to Chris' room. Alex gently sets Chris down so he can pull his room key out. "No one must find out about that."

"Tell that to all the fans that saw you on the way here." I said smiling.

"Well, they won't find it that weird." Chris said.

"Why not?" I asked curiously.

"It's us, we are always caught doing something stupid." Chris said.

"That's because you start it." Alex says as Chris hands me

the keys for his room. I unlock the door and open it. Alex wraps Chris' arm around his shoulders for support while Chris jumps in on his good leg. I hold the door open for them and Chris sits himself on the bed.

"Next time you don't bring these with you, I'm going to hit you with them." I said, grabbing his crutches.

"No, you won't. You're all talk." Chris says as he grits his teeth as he lifts the heavy cast onto the bed.

"Are you trying to rip the stitches out of your scar?" I hurry to his side to help.

"They won't rip. They are still glued together under there." Chris says as he pulls himself up the bed with the help of his other leg.

"Glue doesn't mean anything." I said.

"Are you a doctor?" Alex asked.

"I can't say." I said, smirking.

"She's a paramedic." Chris said.

"Chris, you don't know anything." I said smacking him.

"You haven't told me what you do." Alex said.

"I'm an EMT, a registered nurse, and I have a bachelor's degree in business. I work as a manager in training of health services and EMT response at the Resort. Sometimes I work as an EMT when needed at the training facility." I said.

"She is the person that's always there when I have to get a wheelchair." Chris said.

"I made Chris my special case." I glance over to Chris, and he gives me his goofy smile.

"He certainly is special." Alex says as he crosses his arms over his chest.

I rest my hand on Chris's cast, "Why haven't you had people sign your cast?"

"What for? It'll be cut off soon enough and I won't keep it after that. You know how stinky this thing will be afterwards." Chris said.

"You know, you're probably right. That thing will be stinky." Alex said.

"I dare you to smell it when it gets cut off."

"You're on." Alex said as they shook hands.

"Oh gross." I say, rolling my eyes as I head towards the door. Alex clotheslines me in the abdomen causing me to stop in my tracks.

"Where are you going?" Alex asked.

"Do I need to tell you everything?" I asked.

"Yes, you make him tell you everything." Alex said, pointing to Chris.

"Well, he's different." I said with a smile.

"I'm not different." Chris said offensively.

"I meant a good different." I say as Chris smiles.

"No seriously, where are you going?" Alex asked.

"I'm slightly hungry, so I'm going to go get a snack." I said honestly.

"I'll come with you." Alex said.

"Uh, no." I said.

"Why not?" Alex asked.

"Because…"

"Because why?" Alex asked curiously.

"Because I don't do well eating around people." I said honestly. Alex and Chris burst into laughter, "It's not funny."

"Are you serious?" Chris asked, calming down from laughter.

"Yes, I don't do well eating around people that I don't know that well or trust." I said honestly.

"Why?" Alex asked.

"I don't know, I just get self-conscious about it." I shrugged.

"That is a weird self-conscious issue you have." Chris says and I can tell he is trying not to laugh.

"This is why I don't tell people." I say as I re-open the door heading out. I can hear them burst out in laughter yet again, "Laugh it up guys." I said to myself after the doors had shut.

I went and grabbed a pretzel before taking it up to my room. I let myself into my room, setting my drink onto the nightstand before climbing onto the bed. I got comfortable before I click the television on to watch the designated wrestling channel.

I start eating my food while I enjoy the wrestling matches. I try not to spit food out when I am yelling at the match. A knock sounds at the door, and it starts to open slowly.

"There you are, I was looking for you. Wait, are you uncomfortable? I can leave." Alex says pointing back in his room when he realizes I am eating. He starts to chuckle a tad but clears his throat trying to make sure I didn't hear the chuckles.

"Nah, it's fine. What's up?" I asked, putting my food aside.

"Nothing, I was bored and wanted to see what you were doing." Alex says when his phone begins to ring, "Ugh! Who's calling me now?" Alex asked, pulling out his phone, "I'll be back." Alex said, stepping back into his room. He leaves the door open so I can hear his conversation.

From the sounds of it, he has to replace someone in a match before we anchor for the night near the Mexico coast. We are a tad behind schedule since we were supposed to anchor earlier this afternoon but at least we got to our destination. "Great, Rob's ankle is sprained. They don't want him wrestling on it, so I have to fill in for his match." Alex says, stepping into my room. I cover my mouth as I chew my food.

"You already wrestled today though." I said.

"Yeah, but apparently all the other wrestlers are booked doing other things and I have an open schedule this weekend thanks to Chris."

"Why's that?" I asked.

"Since he's injured, he can't do much and they often pair me with him due to us being a tag team. So, since he can't do much, they have me doing nothing either."

"That must be awesome but also suck." I said.

"Yeah, but after my match I'll be able to head inland if I want or I can stay aboard and attend the ball." Alex said.

"You still have to attend the events though?"

"They highly suggest that us wrestlers do so." Alex said.

"Where are my manners, come and sit." I say pulling my legs into an Indian style so there will be room.

"It's fine, I need to get ready for my match. You want to come down when you finish your pretzel?"

"I'll think about it."

"I'll appreciate it." Alex says before he heads back to his room.

"Alex!" I yell after him. Alex stops in the doorway, turns to look at me and leans against the frame. "Are you going to this 'ball' or are you heading to Mexico?"

"I haven't decided."

"Let me know what you decide."

"Why? Whatever I do, you'll do?" Alex asked.

"No, I'll do the opposite."

"You'll do whatever Chris does, and Chris will do whatever I decide."

"Will not."

"We'll see about that." Alex said as he went into his room

102

shutting the door. I truly want to hate his annoying ways but yet I can't help but to smile and really begin to like his personality. I finish eating my food, I finish the rest of my drink before I turn off my television and head out of the room. I make sure I have everything when I feel my phone vibrating. I pull it out seeing my mom's photo along with her name illuminating.

"Hello?" I say when I pick it up.

"Hey sweetie, how is everything?" My mom asked.

"Great, we are about to anchor at the coast of Mexico. We are a tad behind so I might get in later than usual. I just hope that I can board my flight on time."

"Well, call me when you land, and I will be there in twenty minutes."

"Twenty minutes? Aren't you at your house?" I asked.

"We decided to stay in your house if you don't mind."

"No, not at all."

"The reason I called, Xavier didn't have lice and his back is fine. He has a field trip to Calico next week, can he go?"

"That's great news and I'll transfer cash over for the field trip if they need it."

"I will text the information over. Xavier is staring at me intently wanting the phone," my mom said.

"Hand it to him." I said smiling, this is the longest time I have ever spent away from him and it's hard. Truth be told, thanks to Alex and Chris, I haven't been able to think about Xavier or work.

"Mommy! How's the boat?"

"It's really big and I've gotten lost. The ocean is beautiful."

"Have you seen dolphins? Grandma showed me pictures of dolphins and whales...I got scared of the sharks." Xavier said.

"I'm scared of sharks too. I haven't seen any yet sweetie, but if I do, I will try to snap photos for you." I say stepping onto the elevator seeing a man that towers over me with red hair. He is carrying a gym bag, so I assume he is heading to the gym or getting ready for a match. He smiles at me, and I smile back before I turn around facing the doors that are open.

The doors begin to close a few moments later.

"When are you going to be home, mommy? I miss you."

"I'll be home soon. Are you behaving?"

"Yes! I helped Grandma clean my room."

"Good boy!" I say smiling when the doors open. The guy lets me walk off first and he walks off behind me.

"I like cleaning. I helped fold laundry."

"You're doing real good."

"Yes mommy, ooohhh dinosaurs are on T.V." Xavier says as I hear the phone drop to the floor. I just laugh a tad and roll my eyes when I hear my mom quickly pick up the phone.

"Sorry about that. I hope you don't mind me cleaning up around here."

"It's very much appreciated, Lord knows I don't have the time. Thanks, mom." I said.

"You're welcome. Have fun."

"Will do, love you." I said as I hung up. I slide the phone into my pocket as I walk by a store that sells pretty much anything it looks like.

I walk into the store hoping to make a quick shopping trip for souvenirs. I find a plush dinosaur for Xavier, as well as a few things that my mom and Stephanie would like. I head out of the store and find my way to the ring.

Alex had just climbed to the second turnbuckle yelling something that I couldn't make out due to how far away I was. He sees me, we make eye contact long enough for a smile to creep upon both our faces and he jumps off the turnbuckle. He leans forward against the top turnbuckle just smiling. He doesn't stop staring at me as I feel my cheeks burning from how bad I am blushing.

Another music hit; Alex looks over to the curtain seeing the man I was on the elevator with emerge from behind the curtain. He walks around the barrier giving out high fives to fans before he jumps onto the apron. He gets to his feet, poses for pictures before he climbs between the ropes. He moves to the opposing corner of Alex when the ref signals for the bell to ring.

I stand in the back of the crowd with my arms crossed over my chest. I didn't want to waste the battery on my phone by snapping pictures. I wasn't sure if I would want Xavier to watch this even though I allow him to watch hockey. I watch the way Alex is able to move in the ring, he is very flexible and is very good at aerial tricks.

Unfortunately, the other guy got the pin over him. Alex's opponent has his arm raised in victory before he looks at Alex who is laying in the middle of the ring. The red head climbs out of the ring and heads back behind the curtain. Alex then starts to get up with some help from the ref. I can't tell if he is faking his injuries or if he is truly injured.

Fans begin to clear out to go do other things. I walk to the edge of the boat leaning against the railing to look out at the ocean. I feel my phone going off again and I thought it was my mom yet again. "Hi, mom."

"Hi, daughter." I hear a male voice on the other end say.

"You're not my mom, and this isn't Chris. Who is this?" I pulled out my phone seeing a number I don't recognize displayed on the screen.

"Alex. Where are you?"

"How'd you get my number?" I ask curiously.

"Tell me where you're at and I'll tell you how I got your number."

"I'm on the ship. Now, how'd you get my number?" I asked.

"Good one. No seriously, where are you?"

"I'm on the ship, now seriously how'd you get my number?"

"I stole it from Chris' phone when he was using the bathroom earlier." Alex said.

"Ugh! Dang him for leaving his phone everywhere." I said, rolling my eyes.

"Now, where are you?"

"I'm leaning against the railing across from the curtain." I say as I turn around to look at the curtain. I see the curtain ruffle some before I see him peek out, even though I am far away I can see a smile on his face. I wave slightly, "I see you."

"I see you too, I'll be out in a moment." Alex said.

"Okay." I said as I hung up. I put my phone back in my pocket, turning completely around to watch the curtain.

The curtain opens again a few moments later seeing the black-haired man that I am waiting on. I push myself off the railing, walking towards him to meet him halfway. "Good match."

"Thanks. Sorry, I'm all sweaty and stinky. Do you want to head to Mexico? I think I overheard someone say the boat will be docking in the next half hour." Alex asks as we turn to head to our rooms.

"I would like to. I have never been outside of the United States. I haven't even been to Hawaii or Alaska." I said honestly.

"Seriously?"

"Seriously. I've never been on a plane nor a cruise boat until this trip. I have only been to California because it's within driving distance and my mom lives at the state line." I said.

"You need to travel more."

"Do I?"

"Yes, you can come on tour with us as Chris's assistant." Alex said, smirking.

"Well, I won't be his 'assistant' for long." I said doing air quotes around the word assistant.

"Why?"

"He won't be injured for too much longer." I said as I put my hands in my pockets and Alex clenched his fist on the strap of his duffel bag pushing the strap off his chest.

"Well, you can still go on tour with us. You can be my posse."

"I can't just quit my job and stop everything to go on tour with you guys."

"Why not? What is so special about your job?" Alex asked.

"I enjoy my job; I love what I do. Plus, that is the only thing I know and that is where I'm supposed to be. What is so special about wrestling?"

"I honestly don't know what is so special about wrestling. What made you decide you wanted to be in the medical field, or do the business side of it?"

"I have seen enough injuries in my lifetime, along with illnesses that I learned to enjoy being in hospitals. I love helping people and what better way than to be in the medical field?"

"But that doesn't explain why you are trying to be in the business side of it."

"My dad was a lawyer, my uncles and aunts all own their own businesses. I took a few business classes, and it made me feel smart, opposed to how stupid I truly am."

"You're not that stupid." Alex said, smirking.

"Thanks, but I do my own number of stupid things. What made you decide to wrestle?" I ask curiously as we step up a couple of steps.

"It was destiny, ever since I was a kid watching it on television. I knew that it was where I was going to be."

"You were that kid that would attempt the things at home even if they said not to, huh?"

"Yep, but I was safe about it."

"How can you be safe about it?" I asked, chuckling a tad.

"Attention all cruisers, we are now docked for the night. If you want to head inland, please come on down to the Laredo deck. Ferries will arrive and depart every fifteen minutes until eleven." A man announced over the intercoms throughout the boat. It got Alex and I to stop our conversation for a moment.

"I had adult supervision." Alex said.

"That is so much better. What else do you do besides wrestle?" I asked.

"Chris and I have a band. I love music."

"Me too."

"You have a band?" Alex asked, giving me a questionable look.

"No, I love music." I chuckled. We turn the corner going to the elevator hall.

"Who do you listen to?"

"I'm too embarrassed to say." I say feeling self-conscious if I express my taste in music. I feel we won't have that in common. I want this to work with Alex but feel the more we learn about each other the more I fear we are all wrong for each other.

"I'm not going to judge you based on who you listen to. We all like who we like, and I can't judge you for being who you are." Alex said when a ding chimed before the metal doors opened. We both walk on the elevator shaft. I turn to look back at the doors watching them close. Alex leans forward pressing the number four button.

"How do I know you're not?"

"Do I look like I lie?"

"Yeah." I said jokingly.

"Look, I know that not everyone listens to who I listen to and that no one is perfect. We are all human; we all have flaws. I encourage people to be who they are and do what makes them happy. I don't think it's right to judge people for liking something that may be different." Alex said and that was one of the deepest things I ever heard him say.

"That is the deepest thing I have ever heard a guy say. You just earned a little bit of respect." I nodded approvingly.

"Does that mean I get to know who you listen to now?" Alex asked as a ding chimed, and the doors opened again.

"I like my boy bands, well besides the Jonas Brothers and the newer generation people. I can't handle that Bieber kid." I say as he lets me step off the elevator first and he steps off behind me.

"Most girls do love their boy bands; I have noticed that pattern." Alex says as we walk side by side around the corner to walk down the open corridor to our rooms.

"Pattern? How many girls have you dated?" I asked curiously. If we were to get serious, I should know his dating history.

"Not very many, but Chris has sisters and a few of my other friends had sisters that enjoyed their boy bands. What are their names?" Alex said, tapping his finger against his chin trying to remember.

"Backstreet Boys, NSYNC, and New Kids on the Block are

the ones I mainly obsess about."

"That's it." Alex said, snapping his fingers in the aha moment that it clicked in his mind.

"I have a feeling you don't listen to that type of music."

"No, I'm more of a hardcore rock type person."

"I couldn't tell by the way you dressed." I joke, giving his outfit a look over. For once, he was in gym clothes opposed to his rock star attire. "Do I get brownie points if I say that I listen to Good Charlotte, Green Day, AC/DC, KISS, and Rolling Stones?"

"Eh, those are okay bands."

"Okay?" I asked, throwing my hands on my hips and gasping offensively.

"Fine, those bands are pretty good." Alex said with a smile.

"When will I listen to your music?" I asked as we stopped in front of my door.

"Later. Let me shower up and we will head into Mexico."

"We?" I was kind of happy that he wanted to spend time with me but yet shocked.

"Yeah, that is if you want to hang out with me." Alex said sheepishly.

"Yeah, I would like to hang out with you." I said, smirking.

"I'm happy to hear that. Give me fifteen minutes." Alex said. He walks the short distance to his room; we both unlock our rooms at the same moment. I open my door, hurry in, and push the door shut behind me. I lean back against the door smiling ear to ear, happy that we both want to hang out with each other. He might actually like me, what if he likes me?

Chapter Eleven:

The first thing I do when I get in my room is put a new seasick patch on. I prop the window open to get some fresh air in the room. I pull out my phone storing the number Alex called me on as his contact information. I go to my suitcase tucking the bag of souvenirs into it, seeing Gary the dinosaur still peering out. I pick up the dinosaur, carrying it to the bed where I sit on the edge holding it.

I realize that this is the longest and farthest I have ever been away from my son. Yeah, I have worked night shifts that bled into a day shift at the Resort, but I have not been away from my son for more than a full twenty-four hours. I always made time for him in my daily routine. Even if I were fresh off a twenty-two-hour shift, I would take him to Chuck E Cheese or I would go to the trampoline park. I love Xavier and begin to miss him. I feel guilty that I am even here, I am a mom so I shouldn't be having this much fun.

I run my hand over the back of the dinosaur just smiling. I remembered when he opened this on his fifth birthday last year. *What am I doing? I'm on a boat filled with wrestlers. I know that he is okay with my mom, and he wants me to have fun. It's okay to be homesick but don't worry too much about him, he's fine.* I thought to myself.

I put the dinosaur back into the suitcase to grab my swimsuit. I walk into the bathroom pulling the swimsuit on before pulling my outfit back on over my suit. I head back out to the main room to put my shoes on.

I get comfortable on the bed after tying my shoes. I turn the television on, only for a knock to come to the door. I look at the door. *You gotta be kidding?* I think to myself.

"It's unlocked." I say as the door opens, and Alex leans against the door frame.

"Why aren't you in your bathing suit?"

"I'm wearing it under this." I said, smirking.

"Oh. Are you okay with going to Mexico?" Alex asked.

"If I didn't want to, I wouldn't have gotten into my swimsuit." I say as I turn the television off. I swing my legs over the edge of my bed to stand up.

"Very true." Alex said. I grab my belongings before he holds the door open for me. I walk out onto the open walkway that overlooks the mall area. Alex walks out and pulls the door closed behind him. He tests the door to make sure it is completely shut.

"Do you always test the doors when you leave?" I asked curiously.

"Yeah, I'm very eerie and cautious about those things." Alex said.

"I think I would be too if I stayed in hotels as much as you do." I say as I sheepishly push a strand of hair behind my ear.

"I don't stay in hotels that much. I just don't trust that many people."

"Do you trust me?"

"I have too."

"Why do you have to?" I ask not sure if I am offended or not.

"If Chris trusts you, I trust whoever Chris trusts. Plus, after everything you have gone through already with Chris and I this weekend, I trust you." Alex said as he put his hands in his jacket's pocket.

"Do you always have trust issues?"

"I don't have trust issues, it's just that I don't want to worry about things being stolen. I think trust is earned along with respect besides certain obvious people." Alex said as we turned into the mini hallway. Alex leans forward pressing the down button for the elevator before he stands back up. He zips his zipper up a little more on the leather jacket making it harder to see the black tank top underneath.

"What people instantly have respect?" I asked him curiously.

"The president, I was always taught to respect the president even if you may not have wanted such candidate to win. Military personnel, those people do a lot for this country and go through a lot of stuff that I can't even imagine. And women." Alex said as the elevator tinged before the doors opened. Alex and I climb onto the elevator again. He pushes the main floor level button for us, and the door closes again.

"So, do you use your music to swoon women?" I ask curiously as I lean against the bar that wraps around the elevator.

"That depends." Alex said, smirking.

"Depends on what?" I asked as the elevator came to a stop. We climb off the elevator heading through the mall part to where the ferries are departing.

"If the woman digs that music or likes my voice. I don't have a good voice period."

"I doubt that." I say. I like Alex's deep raspy voice. His voice wasn't as deep as Barry Whites but his voice is definitely attractive. I found his voice attractive at least.

"How would you know? You haven't heard it." Alex says as he bumps into me.

"Do you have some samples with you?" I asked.

"I'll play some songs for you on the ferry ride."

"What's the band called?" I asked curiously.

"The Unknown Spirit." Alex said.

"The Unknown Spirit? Interesting." I say as we get to the end of the ridiculously long line of people that are waiting to be sailed inland.

"I thought so. Do you believe in the paranormal?"

"Paranormal? Somewhat, I watch some of those ghost encounter shows or movies. I usually watch those things when my so-" I said, stopping myself from finishing that word. I bite at my bottom lip. I did not want to finish that word.

"When what?" Alex asked.

"When everyone is asleep at my house. I'm the only one that tends to like that stuff in my house."

"Who all lives in your house?" Alex asked.

"A few people, but I wouldn't change it for the world. I love being around people." I shrugged.

"Me too, but after a while being around certain people, I tend to want to pull my hair out."

"Isn't that why you work the way you work? What is your work schedule?" I asked curiously as a ferry pulled up. People were helped off the ferry before the people in front of us started to get helped into the ferry.

"We film in Vegas on Monday and Tuesday, sometimes we may not film there but somewhere nearby like California. We sometimes travel throughout the rest of the week or over the weekend to other states to please our fans. We also have Pay-Per-Views on Sundays."

"Pay-Per-Views are those big events?"

"Well duh! Pay-Per-Views are events that people have to pay to view and it's usually the big matches that are too special for our weekly broadcast." Alex explained as we moved further up the line. A second ferry arrives that we are able to board. "Ladies first."

Alex offers his hand for support as I have to step the distance between the cruise ship and the ferry. I was able to step the distance and had to step down a few steps. I get to the bottom looking up at Alex who has to step over the distance between the cruise ship and the ferry.

I claim an empty spot on the ferry for Alex and me to sit. The boat seems filled and crowded compared to how the cruise ship felt.

"Hey, it's Alex Johnson!" A kid said, pointing towards us excitedly.

"Hey guys! How is everyone? I hope you all are enjoying the cruise thus far." Alex says, waving as he heads towards me. Everyone mumbles out their 'goods,' or their 'greats,' in response to Alex's question. Alex sits down beside me, and he leans back against the back of the boat.

"I'm having a horrible time." I said trying to fight a smile that was threatening to come on my face.

"You're such a liar." Alex says poking my side, which is my ticklish spot unfortunately and it makes me squirm. "Is that a ticklish spot?"

"No," I lie, "You guys have a weekly broadcast?" Hoping to change the subject so he will stop tickling me.

"Yep, every Thursday night on SyFy." Alex says as he pulls out his iPhone, "I didn't grab my ear buds."

"I have mine." I say pulling my purse onto my lap. I zip it open. Alex leans over to try and look into my purse. Tugging my purse out of his eyesight, "Do you mind?"

"Sorry. I'm nosey." Alex says when I pull out my ear buds along with a pack of gum.

"You want some?" I offer him a piece as I am already unwrapping a piece for myself.

"Yes, please." Alex said, grabbing a piece for himself. He unwraps it before he tosses it into his mouth.

"I hope you don't mind the buds." I say as I put the purse back down between my feet before turning my focus to untangling the earbuds cord.

"No, not at all. Wait, are those skulls on the buds?" Alex asked, grabbing one of the buds.

"Yeah, why?"

"That's awesome."

"I got them at Walgreens. Who knew they had something that awesome, huh?" I said as he was amused with it.

"I have to go get a pair like this; I dig it." Alex says as he plugs them into his iPhone. He begins searching for something on his phone while I finish untangling the buds.

I stick the bud into my ear to listen in on what Alex chose to play. Alex plays a song that I have never heard before, I don't bother to ask about the song. I figure I will ask questions after so I can give the song a full listen.

The song is totally the type of song I would head bang to, Alex and I listen to song after song until we arrive at the dock.

We wait our turn to get off the boat. I step aside letting fans take their pictures with Alex, which I didn't mind. I entertain myself by taking pictures with my phone to send to my mom later.

"How do you feel being out of the United States for the first time?" Alex asked, stepping up beside me.

"Feels the same as being in the United States." I said.

"It always does. Well, unless you go into the cities, and no one speaks English, then it's a little tough."

"Have you learned any other language besides English?" I ask as we walk down the wooden dock towards the beach.

"I know a little of everything. I had to learn a few words when we went overseas. We usually stay overseas for a few days. You need to survive somehow."

"Do you know sign language?" I asked curiously.

"Never learned that. What about you?" Alex asks as we step down a couple steps onto the sand.

"I know Spanish, I had to learn it for my job. I know sign language as well."

"When did you learn sign language?"

"I was taught at a young age. Well, at least the alphabet and as I got older the more interested I got." I said.

"Did your mom teach you?"

"She taught me the alphabet."

"Why did she teach you?" Alex asks as he stops and sits on the beach. He pats the spot beside him for me to sit beside him. I slowly sit down beside him to look out at the ocean that had waves crashing into the sand in front of us.

"My grandpa was deaf. My mom, aunt, uncle, and grandma all had to learn sign language to communicate with him. I kind of wanted to learn so I could have a relationship with him."

"That sucks…I think if I was going to lose any of my senses, I would want it to be taste." Alex said.

"Me too. Lord knows there are some tastes out there that I can go without tasting and it'll be nice not to have to taste it anymore."

"Like medicine, I hated those dang cough syrups when I was a kid."

"Didn't we all." I said laughing. Xavier hates cough syrups as well so it must be a kid thing.

"When we were kids, we never understood that the stuff would help us. That and vegetables."

"I still don't like some vegetables. Fruits I can deal with." I said.

"What is your favorite fruit?"

"Banana's, I can eat those all the time." I say honestly when I look at the sand seeing a seashell. I pick it up and start cleaning out the sand.

"Do you collect seashells?"

"No. When I was a kid, my mom would do a yearly family trip to California. One of the days on the trip would be spent at the beach. My sister and I would run up and down the beach collecting seashells just to look at the different shapes, colors and just to look at them." I glance over at him smirking.

"Seashells are beautiful things, but I know one thing, well person, who is way more beautiful." Alex says and I feel my cheeks burning from blushing because I presume he means me.

My phone starts to blare through my pocket, I pull it out trying to make sure it doesn't ruin this moment more than it already has. When I get my phone out completely, I see Chris's name. "Who is it?"

"Chris." I say as I answer the call, pressing the phone up to my ear, "Hello?"

"Hey, what are you up to?"

"I'm sitting on the beach."

"Ugh! Is Alex there with you?"

"Yeah, do you need to talk to him?" I ask looking over to Alex who is staring out at the ocean in front of us.

"Nah, just come back and get me."

"Chris, I don't think it's a good idea for you to come to the beach."

"I can sit on the dock. I hate being locked up in this room all weekend long."

"Fine, we'll come back and get you. No swimming!" I said sternly.

"I won't." Chris says as I hang up the phone.

"So?" Alex asked.

"Chris wants us to go back and get him. He's bored and wants to come inland." I say as he rolls his eyes. He stands up and helps me to my feet so we can head back to the dock.

"Here." Alex says as I look over at the sound of his voice. He picks up the seashell and hands it to me, "Take it with you to remind you of this trip and memories of your sister."

"Thanks." I said.

"No problem. Here, let me take a picture of you with it to send to mom." Alex said, offering his hand out for my phone.

"Why don't we take a picture together?" I ask nervously, I hope it wasn't pushy.

"Wouldn't that creep your mom out?" Alex asked.

"It'll keep the impression up that it's a single's cruise." I lie.

"Oh." Alex says as he steps closer. I wrap an arm around him, and he wraps his arm around my waist. I snap a photo of us with the ocean and the lowering sun in the background. "How'd it turn out?" Alex asks curiously. I show him the picture that we just took.

We get to the bottom of the steps that lead up to the dock. He holds onto my hand to help me up the steps which I didn't need but it's still a gentleman's move.

"Are you guys going to do this cruise every year?" I ask as we walk down the dock to where we were dropped off no more than an hour earlier.

"This is our first cruise, I guess there may be more depending how well this plays out. " Alex answered. We stand at the end of the dock, I wrap my arms over my chest trying not to show that I am cold. The ferry arrives with about three people on it, we let them climb out first before we climb aboard. We have the whole ferry to ourselves, so we sit across from each other. "What boat do you prefer, this one or the cruise boat?"

"The cruise boat." I say holding onto the seats beside me.

"Why?"

"This boat makes me nervous." I say as it is rocking with each wave we hit.

"You're not going to like boats after this, are you?"

"Probably not." I said smiling.

"You'll get used to it."

"I'm not on boats often so I don't think I'll ever get used to it."

"You will if you slowly work at it."

"Are you a specialist for curing fears?" I ask sarcastically.

"Little do you know."

"Bull crap, I'm calling bull crap right now." I stop him before he continues.

"You think I will make stuff up?" Alex asks, putting on a

shocked face.

"Yes. You're good friends with Chris and he's known for that type of stuff." I said.

"What has Chris tried to pull on you?"

"I'm not stupid, so I caught him in the act of all his bull crap."

"I bet. He isn't that good of a liar compared to me. "

"Do you lie a lot in order to perfect it?" I ask as the boat comes to a stop, letting us climb onto the larger boat. I walk up to step from the ferry to the cruise ship. I try to do it myself, but the distance between the two boats is too wide for me. I feel myself losing my balance, my arms flailing like that would help me catch my balance.

"Whoa there!" Alex said, his arms snaking around me to hold me still. I feel myself steadying out, looking over my shoulder at Alex embarrassed. "You almost fell into the ocean below."

"I know, that would have sucked." I say as he loosens his grip so I can step the rest of the way onto the cruise ship.

"You said before that your sister almost drowned from jumping off a boat, did you jump in too?" Alex asked, he remembered that?

"I dived in after her to pull her to the surface. The trip wasn't that good after that honestly. Luckily, it was only at Lake Mead, so we hadn't traveled far on the trip."

"Fortunately for that."

"You're from Michigan, were you always on the lake? Isn't Michigan surrounded by lakes?"

"Yes, it is but I don't go on the lake as often as you would think. It isn't much of my style." He shrugged.

"Then what did your family do that was fun growing up?" I ask, he sighs as if he is trying to think.

"We hunted, camped and mostly did a lot of sports."

"Sports family? I'm honestly not so shocked."

"I know, it isn't surprising considering my career." He laughs as we turn down the hall to go towards Chris' room.

"How did you meet Chris?"

"We actually met in school, went through wrestling training and everything together."

"You were friends before you even started wrestling?"

"Yeah, we clicked outside of wrestling and in wrestling our styles clicked. For whatever reason, we just are on the same wavelength. I think that makes us one of the best tag teams."

"Do you wrestle at places other than Pure Gold?"

"Sometimes, I have to go where the money is."

"Do you prefer Las Vegas or Michigan?" I asked curiously.

"I like them both equally for different reasons." Alex said, leave it to him to find the most mutual answer to respond with. "You do know you may have to go to Michigan."

"And why is that?"

"To meet my mom."

"And why would I meet your mom?" I asked with a smile.

"I'm going to meet your mom, and it's only fair. Parents have to approve whatever this is." Alex says, turning to look at the purplish-blue door we have approached. I don't respond, what is he even implying? Is there something between us already? I certainly have started to feel myself falling for him, are the feelings mutual though? I have a feeling they are based on that statement but fear that I will get hurt in the end.

Chapter Twelve:

We stand in front of the purplish-blue door; my mind is flustered from Alex wanting me to meet his parents. Alex reaches forward rhythmically tapping his fist against the door. I feel sheepish standing there beside Alex, I keep glancing over to him and he just stares forward at the door.

"One moment!" Chris yells from the other side of the door before a string of curse words. A few thuds come from inside the room then the door is pulled open.

"Are you okay?" I ask with a raised brow.

"Yeah, fine." Chris said. I can tell that something happened, and he doesn't want to admit it.

"Are you ready to go?" Alex asks.

"Yeah." Chris said excitedly. I feel horrible that he had to come on this cruise, and he is pretty much bound to his room because there isn't much for him to do with a bum leg. Alex and I step apart to give him room to hobble out. I lean in to shut the door for him.

"Are you going to be able to step over to the ferry?" I ask, turning around and heading back to where Alex and I had just come from.

"Psh! I'm perfectly able to step across the gap. Cast be darned." Chris said.

"I told her about our band." Alex said.

"How'd you like it?" Chris asked curiously.

"It was pretty good."

"Pretty good?" Alex asked offensively.

"Fine, it was amazing. Better?" I asked him.

"Much." Alex said.

"Would you like to buy a CD?" Chris asked.

"Not now. Maybe next week when I see you." I said.

"Okay, I'll make sure I'll grab one before I come in." Chris said.

"Do you guys have each other penciled into each other's calendars?" Alex asked.

"No, but like you said you guys perform every Monday and Tuesday at certain times. It never fails, Chris is always in my office at the same time on the same days of every week." I explained.

"It is always during her lunch break too." Chris said, chuckling.

"That's because you found out when my lunch break was and became a jerk about showing up at that time." I said.

"It was quite entertaining at first seeing you get pissed at me about having to miss your lunch break." Chris said. We arrive at the ferry line that is now much shorter than it was earlier.

We stand in the short line waiting our turn to step into the much smaller boat to go inland.

"When do we have to be back?" Alex asked.

"I think the last boat back is at eleven." I say honestly as Alex starts messing with his gold watch on his wrist.

"What time is it now?" Chris asked.

"About six." Alex said. I look out to the sunset to see if that seems accurate. Based on where the sun is resting, I'm sure it was. I turn back around realizing that Alex has his phone up taking a picture of the three of us.

"What the heck? You could have told me you were taking a picture?" I nudge him.

"No, because that'll be too easy." Alex said smiling. He begins to type on his phone, he is probably going to text it to Chris and I or to his family.

"Don't we have that ball thing tonight?" Chris asks, I forgot there was even a ball because I was distracted by Alex this whole trip. I was racking my brain if I had even packed proper attire to wear to a ball. I don't think I did because I didn't have any dresses in my wardrobe to bring and I never went shopping for a dress, so I guess I didn't have anything packed.

"That should be starting right about now if you were to get dinner. I think the actual party starts at eight." Alex said. The ferry stops in front of us and the family of four that are occupying the boat steps onto the cruise ship with us. I look at the gap between the cruise ship and the ferry, I become worried how Chris is going to get onto the smaller boat.

"I'm going to love seeing you trying to step over. I almost fell in once and I don't have a casted leg." I say looking down at the ocean below us in the gap between boats.

"That's why you're here to help support me and I got Alex too." Chris said with an evil smile.

"Boy, do I feel the love." I roll my eyes stepping beside him. He pulls out the crutches and hands them over to the employee. Alex and I hold onto Chris by his upper arms for support as he steps over the gap and onto the ferry. At least he stepped forward on his good leg, he swung his bad leg over. The employee hands Chris the crutches and he stuffs them back under his armpits.

"You are so crazy." I said not believing that he was going into Mexico or going to the dock. Having the cast on his leg, he shouldn't be doing any of this because it wasn't safe. What was I thinking? I'm not at work so I need to let my medical knowledge slip from my mind and let Chris live his life. Alex steps over and goes to sit beside Chris, I lean against the metal edge of the door staring at the two men I am going inland with.

I couldn't believe what has come from this cruise and it has not been what I had expected it to be. I didn't know what to expect coming onto a 'singles' cruise, a smile creeping onto my face thinking of all the fun I have been having. *I secretly am happy I met Alex, I think I would have been miserable and lost on the cruise not having Stephanie here to be my partner in crime. When she bailed, I honestly planned to just lounging in my room the whole time.*

"Come on, Tara!" Alex yells, snapping me out of my thoughts. I take a deep breath and step over the threshold onto the ferry. When I get onto the ferry, I walk over to the two men that are talking among themselves. I slide into the seat beside Chris trying to listen in on what is being discussed.

"Why are you sitting next to him?" Alex asked.

"Because he smells better." I said.

"Thank you." Chris said, taking it as a compliment.

"We are going to make a Tara sandwich." Alex says as he stands up and moves to sit on the other side of me.

"I do not like this." I said.

126

"Why not? Are you uncomfortable?" Alex asked.

"Yes, this is very uncomfortable." I said.

"We can make it more uncomfortable." Chris says as they both start scooting closer to me, squishing me between them.

"Stop it!" I say as I try to push them away, but they keep scooting in. I eventually stand up and move to the other end of the boat.

"You're no fun." Chris yells with a pout.

"I am fun." I say defensively.

"Prove it." Alex says.

"How do you prove that?"

"Move back over here."

"Fine." I stand up and walk back over to them. I sit down between them, hoping they won't try to scoot in again.

"Much better." Alex says as he rests his arm behind me.

"I don't get how sitting here is better." I say with a shrug.

"Because Alex likes you." Chris says nonchalantly. I look from Chris to Alex who can't make eye contact with me, his stare is out into the miles of ocean ahead of us.

"Shut up, Chris." Alex said, smacking Chris on his bicep.

"What? Like it isn't true." Chris said with a shrug.

"Land ahoy!" The captain says breaking the conversation and the uncomfortable tension between us. I can't stop thinking of what Chris just said, and I keep glancing over to Alex with a smile. *Alex likes me? I like him too. Maybe it is mutual between us.* I bite at my bottom lip as the captain docked us next to the wood dock.

"Land!" Chris said in excitement.

"Calm down, woman!" Alex said jokingly. Alex stands up first then sticks his hand out to help me to my feet. I smile at the gesture, it is very sweet.

"Dude! What about me?" Chris asks as I take Alex's hand.

"Ladies first." Alex said, winking towards me.

"Whatever." Chris said. We both help pull Chris to his feet and follow him over to the short ladder that hooks onto the dock. Alex climbs up first with the crutches as Chris pulls himself up the ladder.

"Be careful." I say in a worried tone. I watch Chris pull himself up and onto the dock.

"Like always. And that's why you're below me to catch me if I fall." Chris said, looking down at me with a smile.

"Chris, seriously." I say as he laughs before he swings his leg over the ladder to pull himself to a stand on the dock. Alex hands Chris the crutches.

"I swear he's going to give me a heart attack." I mumble to myself. I begin to climb the ladder and get towards the top of the ladder seeing a hand being lowered into my eyesight.

"Let me help you." Alex said.

"Thanks." I said taking his hand as an offering to help.

"When did you become a gentleman?" Chris jokes as Alex helps me onto the dock.

"I'm always a gentleman." Alex responds as I begin to help Chris sit down on the edge of the dock. "I thought you wanted to go back to the beach?" Alex asks, pointing to the beach below with his thumb.

"Chris can't. His cast nor his crutches will allow for it. We'll stick here." I say but Alex started to pout, "Alex, it's fine." I say with a reassuring smile and sit beside Chris. I put the crutches behind us, Alex sighs before he sits down beside Chris.

"If only it was darker, then I will be able to dazzle you with my ability to find the zodiac signs." Alex says, he is staring up at the darker sky.

"I was never good at finding the zodiac signs nor the constellations like the dippers or the North Star." I admit.

"Have you ever tried counting the stars? There are so many of them." Chris said.

"I have never swam in the moonlight." Alex said randomly.

"Me neither." Chris said.

"I dare you to jump in." Alex said.

"Chris, you can't." I said, grabbing Chris's arm.

"Why not? My cast? What's the worst thing that is going to happen?"

"You'll have to get a new cast and your scar may get infected."

"Would that delay my healing?"

"Who cares? Dive on in." Alex nudged Chris a tad.

"I do." Chris said. Alex rolls his eyes and jokingly pushes Chris. Chris slides off the wood planks, hearing him scream as he falls the distance between the dock and the ocean. A big splash from when he submerged into the giant body of water.

"Alex! He can't swim due to the weight of the cast!" I yell angrily. I jump to my feet, quickly strip down to my swimsuit and dove in after Chris. I swim further down until I see Chris floating slowly down. I wrap my arms around Chris' helpless body and pull him with me to the surface. Chris is gasping to catch his breath and I am dragging him towards the dock.

"You're such a jerk." Chris finally is able to say.

"Oops." Alex says with laughter. Chris splashes Alex from where we are.

"You're such a jerk man." Chris says.

"We need to get you back to the cruise ship, ASAP." I am worried about Chris's cast and scar. I help him up the ladder and pick up my clothes that are piled up. I pull them on quickly trying to escort Chris back to the ferry.

"You seriously are no fun." Alex said.

"Don't talk to me Alex." I snapped.

"OooohhH!" Chris said as he pushed his now wet hair out of his face.

"What's your issue?" Alex asked.

"You. I'm really miffed at you for not listening to me. Why would you push your best friend into the ocean knowing that he can't swim? He could have died. Now, we have bigger issues. His scar can get infected, and his cast is going to shrink. It can delay his healing. It's like you don't even care, it's all about fun for you, isn't it?" I ramble on angrily.

"I was joking!" Alex said.

"Joking or not, it was very rude and disrespectful." I said. I help Chris towards the end of the dock to board the ferry. Alex locks his jaw; I can sense how angry he is from me standing up to him over his actions. The ferry pulls up. I help Chris down and Alex boards behind us. I get Chris situated before turning to the driver, "Can you go fast? We need to get him to the first aide office."

"Yes, ma'am." The captain says with a nod. He heads to the wheel to steer the ferry back towards the cruise. Alex sits at the opposite end of the boat ignoring us completely. I sit down beside Chris checking his cast for any drying spots but there isn't any as of yet.

Chapter Thirteen:

We get to the cruise ship just in time, I grab Chris's crutches bringing them to him. I glance over at Alex who is still sitting at the other end of the boat. Alex still has his arms crossed over his chest and jaw locked, obvious signs that he is still pissed off.

"Don't worry about him, he's not used to being snapped at." Chris whispers.

"I didn't mean to snap." I say softly. I am upset that I angered Alex, but he had to be told.

"I know." Chris said.

"You need help, ma'am?" The employee asks as he holds out his hand.

"Yes, please." I say as I accept his hand, and he helps me step over to the cruise ship. I turn around being handed Chris's crutches. The captain helps Chris maneuver himself across the gap without falling in yet again. I hand Chris the crutches, he slides them under his armpits and begins to slide past me. I offer my hand towards Alex who is now ready to board the cruise ship again. Alex ignores my hand, stepping onto the cruise and stands toe to toe with me. I look up into his brown eyes, I can see the hurt and anger in his eyes. He pushes past me, my eyes following him as he slides past Chris to walk away. I cross my arms over my chest making myself further upset.

"Alex, dude! You don't have to ignore the lady; she was trying to help and protect me." Chris yells after Alex.

Alex waves his hand in the air, "Whatever man."

"Don't worry about him, he'll get over it. Let's worry about my leg, I think the cast is drying." Chris said in a monotone.

"Yeah, let's hurry." I say as we try to find a map of the ship. We find our way to first aide, I push the door open and hold it open while he hobbles in. Chris begins to wince in pain from the drying cast, which causes the cast to shrink. I'm sure there is some stinging from the salt water on his scar, which probably didn't help him in the uncomfortable factor.

"What's wrong?" The nurse asks.

"Chris here went into the ocean with his cast. He needs a new one or a splint along with rinsing his scar out." I state.

"Alright, Chris come on over here. I'll call the doctor down." She said helping Chris to one of the two beds they had. I check my phone seeing it was seven now.

"You can leave if you want." Chris said. I slide my phone back into my pocket and walk over to stand beside him.

"And leave you?" I ask, putting on a fake smile. I was trying to put my worries and feelings about Alex aside. I need to focus on Chris's health.

"Why do you care about me so much?" Chris asked.

"You haven't given me a reason not to. Once a patient, always a patient."

"I would hug you but I'm in pain." Chris says as the lady rolls me a seat and I sit down holding Chris's hand. "Why are you holding my hand?"

"For you to squeeze when you have pain." I said.

"I'm a big boy and I'm not pregnant with contractions." Chris jokes when the door is pushed open. A man walks into the room.

"What do we have here?" He asked while he walked by us to go wash his hands and pulls a new set of latex gloves on.

"I got pushed into the ocean. My scar stings and the cast feels like it's tightening." Chris explained.

"Let's see what we can do." He says as he pulls out his saw and begins cutting off the old cast.

"If only Alex were here to smell it." Chris said, chuckling.

"He can smell the other one." I said, rolling my eyes. That is what he is most concerned about. The doctor begins to spray water over the stitched up part of his leg. He pats it dry before wiping it over with an antiseptic wipe.

"That is all I could do as far as cleaning it out, I can't cast it. All I can do is put a splint on it. If I do a splint, you have to move a lot slower and try your best to stay off of it." The doctor instructed.

"So, you just might have to get that wheelchair you have been fighting against." I said smiling.

"That might be the best if you want to be moving around for long distances." The doctor said pulling a chair up to the bed. He instructs the nurse on what materials to grab. She brings all the proper tools to the bedside. I watch as the doctor begins to put the splint over Chris's leg.

"Do I have to?" Chris whined and I couldn't help but to laugh.

"Yes, you can thank Alex for being stupid." I said.

"Katie, can you get a wheelchair for me?" The doctor asks, the nurse nods before retrieving the wheelchair. "When you get on land, you will have to go to your doctor to get a new cast put on for the remainder of time."

"He will." I said.

"Am I?" Chris asked, looking at me with a perked brow. I nod and he looks back at the doctor, "I guess I am."

"Well, have them check and make sure your scar isn't infected. We don't want that." He says as I help hold Chris's leg still as the doctor finishes wrapping the splint on Chris's leg. The nurse comes back in with a wheelchair and rolls it over to us, Chris moves himself over to the wheelchair and I prop his leg up onto the leg extender.

"I thought I would have a few days break from my throne on wheels, but I guess not." Chris sighed as he rubs at the arm rests.

"I think it missed you more than you missed it." I joke as I twirl him around to head out of the office. "Are you hungry?" I ask as I begin to push him towards the food court.

"I could eat but I'll get room service. I don't want to burden you." Chris said.

"You're not a burden." I corrected.

"I feel like it. I want you to have the option to go to the ball and have fun without Alex or I. Plus, you need to dry yourself off." Chris says so we head in a different direction to go to his room.

"If I leave you alone tonight, will you let me baby you tomorrow?" I asked stepping in front of him.

"Yes, have fun for me tonight." He said smiling.

"I will, where's your key?" I ask as he digs into his pocket and hands the key over to me. I unlock the door pushing it open and hold the door open for Chris. He rolls himself into the room and over to his bed. I lock the wheels watching him move himself onto the bed and I move his crutches aside. I help him prop his leg up on top of some pillows before I wheeled the wheelchair out of the common walk ways, so it won't in his way. "Call me, and you better not hesitate on doing so."

"I won't." Chris said smiling. I head out of his room and lean back against his door. Now that I am done worrying about Chris, I have to worry about my relationship with Alex. I'm not even sure if there is a relationship between us.

I don't stop to get my own dinner because I am so worried that I can't eat. I walk up to my room trying not to let my worries eat me alive, but they were. I go into the bathroom changing into my pajamas and hang my swimsuit over the curtain rod. I walk out tossing my dirty clothes on top of my suitcase not even wanting to put them up.

I climb onto the slender bed trying to get comfortable. When I finally get into the perfect comfortable position, I hear a knock. I was confused as to who would be knocking at my door. Alex hates me, Chris wouldn't be able to make it up here in the wheelchair and I don't know anyone else on this boat. I get up from the bed with a huff and make my way to the main door. I look out the peephole to emptiness, no one is there. I instantly knew that it must be Alex knocking at the connecting door. I slowly go to the door and timidly open it, afraid for Alex to see me in my pajamas.

"Alex?" I asked softly, peeking around the door to look at him. Alex has his hair gelled back, he is wearing a black shirt that has a tux top printed on it with both his black zip up hoodie and leather jacket over it. To top off his ensemble, he is wearing a form fitting pair of jeans and leather boots. He is looking down at a lit up rose that he is holding in his hand. He must have bought the rose from the souvenir shop downstairs because I saw it there earlier.

"I'm sorry about earlier. I have never had someone snap at me and I did some thinking. I understand why you were mad. I'll apologize to Chris tomorrow because I put his health at risk. I hope you will accept this rose out of the kindness of your heart and I would love for you to accompany me to the ball. I would hate to waste the rest of the night alone due to my stupidity." Alex says sincerely and offers me the rose. He looks up at me. Our eyes connect, I can see the sincerity and guilt in his eyes.

"I don't have any formal clothes." I say, stepping out from behind my door.

"This is as formal as I get." Alex states as he looks down at his outfit of choice.

"Let me change then." I said excitedly. I grab a new outfit that I think will suit this event. A pair of jeans and a red blouse with off the shoulder long sleeves. I hurry into the bathroom to change and freshen up. I walk out of the bathroom seeing Alex laying on my bed flipping through the channels, "Don't get too comfortable on my behalf." I joke as I slide my feet into some sandals.

"I won't." He said with a smile. He clicks the television off before he hops off the bed. I grab my belongings, and now I am truly ready to leave. Alex finally hands me the rose and I carry it out of the room with us. Alex shoves his hands into the pockets of his leather jacket, "How's Chris?"

"He's confined to a wheelchair for the rest of the trip. When we get back to Vegas, he has to go to his doctor to get a new cast put on. The doctors will probably have to do a deep cleaning of the scar tissues since all they could do was rinse it out and use antiseptic wipe." I responded.

"Can he get infections just from the salt water?"

"Yep. If bacteria from that water gets into his unhealed scar it can cause infections and other issues. Hence why people with casts need to protect such things." I nudge Alex.

"Why'd you stop at nurse and EMT? Don't you want to be a doctor?" Alex asks while he presses the down button for the elevator.

"I do but I don't want to do more work than I already am. I work eighteen plus hours a day and don't want to add schoolwork to the mix."

"Maybe you should work with Pure Gold as our personal trainer to make sure we are physically capable of performing. That'll free up a bunch of time so you can go for that doctorate." Alex suggests.

"After this weekend, I don't know if I can handle it." I joke as we climb onto the elevator that has just opened in front of us.

"What do you mean by that?" Alex asked.

"I won't get work done with you and Chris wandering around."

"Am I distracting?" Alex asked, smirking.

"In a good way." I said twirling the rose between my fingertips.

"You look absolutely beautiful." Alex states as I blush, and can't make eye contact.

"I try."

"You don't have to try, you're naturally beautiful." Alex added.

"I doubt that." I mumble as we walk off the elevator, finally realizing how cold it is, "It's kind of chilly out."

"Well, we are in the middle of the ocean." Alex said sarcastically.

"I know that." I said as I let him lead me to the banquet hall. I hear the music getting louder as we are getting closer. "Aren't we a little under dressed?" I asked Alex, stopping him from going in. I look at the doors then I look at Alex feeling self-conscious about my outfit choice.

"Trust me when I say, we aren't going to be the only ones in jeans." Alex says as he opens the door allowing me to slowly step into the room with him right behind me. "Exhibit A." Alex says, nodding towards Jim who is crossing our path at that exact moment. Jim is wearing a tank top, skintight jeans, and a cowboy hat with a beer in hand.

"Could his jeans be any tighter?" I whispered.

"Yes, they can and it's not pretty. Come on, let's find a seat." Alex said, grabbing my hand leading me to a table that sat two people. He pulls out my chair and pushes it in while I sit down before he sits across from me.

"Um, I think this is a buffet dinner." I notice the long tables of food and people that are serving themselves.

"Oh, right." Alex says, then we stand up taking our plates to the buffet lines. "What's this?" Alex asks as he stirs a noodle dish.

"I don't know. I don't want this. If it still has eyes, I will never grab it." I said looking at a dish with fish that still has eyes staring back at me.

"A good rule to live by." Alex said.

"I thought so. As far as meat goes, I always do well done."

"Me too, I don't like the vampire feeling with all that blood otherwise." Alex said as I put salad on my plate. "You're only getting a salad?"

"I don't see much of anything else I want." I state.

"Dude, they got cinnamon rolls...cinnamon rolls!" Alex said excitedly.

"I'll have one." I say, as he put one on my plate, "Sweets are my downfall." I say as I grab a cup of lemonade. I walk back to our table.

"I love cinnamon rolls, but I usually only have them around the holidays."

"Why's that?" I ask moving my napkin to my lap after crossing my legs at my ankles.

"My mom makes them homemade for every holiday that I come home."

"Why is food so much better when it's homemade?"

"I don't know why it tastes so much better. What is your signature dish?" Alex ask as I take a bite of my salad.

"I think mine would be grilled peanut butter and jelly, I'm told it's to die for." I said.

"Did you say grilled peanut butter and jelly?" Alex asked.

"Yeah, it tastes pretty good."

"I may have to try that. I have a killer recipe for lasagna." Alex said.

"You like to cook?"

"I do but I don't have a lot of people to cook for. I also don't want the guys to know because if they find out then I won't hear the end of it."

"I should hire you as a cook, I never seem to find time to cook."

"I may consider it." Alex says before he takes a sip of his drink.

"Who said I was actually going to hire you?" I asked.

"I took it as an offer." Alex says and I can tell he is a little offended.

"It could be though." I say before I take another bite of my salad. Alex smiles as he takes a bite of his food while a slow song comes on. Jim walks up to our table with his beer still in hand.

"Sorry to interrupt your feast but I was curious if this pretty little lady would give me the privilege of dancing with me." He said. I look at Alex, unsure if I should say yes or no, I'm not sure if this is a date or how he feels.

"I don't mind." Alex says as he looks at me, even though his facial expression says differently.

"Sure, why not?" I say standing up and walking with Jim to the dance floor. I place my one hand on his shoulder, and he rests his hand on my waist while our other hands connect. We dance for a few seconds not speaking to each other during that time.

"I'm not ruining anything, am I?" Jim asked.

"No, why?" I asked nervously.

"Well because we haven't spoken this whole song. Between you and I, I think you and Alex have feelings for each other."

"Why do you say that?" I asked curiously.

"This whole time you keep glancing at him with googly eyes."

"I do not have googly eyes." I said chuckling.

"I have a daughter; I know that look."

"How old is your daughter?" I ask curiously and try to change the subject.

"She'll be six next month, you have kids?"

I sigh looking into Jim's eyes, "It's complicated, Jim." I respond, glancing back to the table, Alex is gone. Where could he have gone?

"How is it complicated?" Jim asks when I feel a tap on my

shoulder.

I look over my shoulder seeing Alex, "May I cut in?" Alex steps up beside us, glancing between Jim and me. I look over at Alex, kind of shocked he is actually asking me to dance but I was nothing but smiles from happiness. His face lights up with a smile when I nod my head yes.

"Yeah, sure." Jim said as he let Alex step in his spot. Alex seems kind of awkward and I know I feel just as awkward for no apparent reason. I was comfortable around Jim.

Alex nervously reaches out grabbing my right hand and resting his other on my hip, he pulls me a little closer to him. We start to slowly rock to the beat of the song. The song comes to a stop no more than ten seconds later, and we instantly let go of each other backing up a tad. He scratches the back of his head feeling more awkward. The DJ then puts on a song by the Backstreet Boys. Alex turns to head back to the table. I grab his arm, turning him back around.

"Where are you going? I thought you wanted to dance?" I said.

"I do but I'm not good at-" He begins before I interrupt.

"No one is good at dancing but it's my jam, please?"

"Okay. Isn't this your band?"

"Yeah, hence why it's my jam." I say smiling. I start to break into their choreographed dance that they do in concert, "Alex, you got to thrust more."

"What?" Alex asks as he stops.

"Look at Jim." I say looking over to Jim who is nailing the dance.

"How the heck do you know this dance?" Alex asked towards Jim.

"I have a wife and a six-year-old who is obsessed with every boy band alive." Jim answered.

"I bet he enjoys it too." Alex whispers. He grabs my hand interlacing his fingers with mine and he gives me a twirl before I spin into his embrace. I smile over my shoulder at Alex, our faces are mere inches apart. Alex pushes me to untwist our arms that were twisted up like a pretzel.

"How'd you know that?" I ask as our hands are still locked together and I step in front of him, locking our other hands together.

"I know a little bit of dancing, I'm just not good at it." He says smiling as he pulls me closer to him.

"I figured you'd be good considering you're in a band and can recognize the beats to the song."

"I got beat, just not rhythm." He says as we both begin rocking to the beat until the end of the song. I gave up trying to teach him the dance moves. "Maybe you can teach me those moves, what was it?" Alex asked, breaking our hand lock to try to mock my moves earlier. I cover my face from embarrassment but I'm laughing. "Was I close?"

"Somewhat." I say as we dance for what seems like hours. I am leaning my head on his shoulder, my hands lying flat on his chest. I feel my eyes getting heavy and his arms are wrapped around my waist tightly.

"Are you ready to leave?" Alex whispered, feeling his breath rustling in my hair. I lift my head off his shoulder looking deep into his hazel eyes.

"Yeah, sorry." I said, rubbing at my eyes.

"No problem, sweetie." Alex said.

"Sweetie?" I was shocked.

"You let Jim call you it."

"But he's Jim." I say smiling as we grab our things. We head out of the room, the night chill sends shivers down my body. Rubbing my hands over my biceps trying to warm myself up some, hoping to make it to my room without my teeth chattering. "Br, it's cold."

"Here, take my jacket." Alex said. He takes his leather jacket off and wraps it around my body. The jacket rests on my shoulders, and I pull the edges closed with my opposing hands.

"Thanks." I said smiling.

"No problem." Alex said with a wink.

"I'm sorry about earlier." I blurt out.

"Don't be sorry, you were right. I was being a jerk and I should have listened to you. People don't do that to their friends."

"I know you were playing around. I don't want to get between you and Chris." I say as we step up a couple of steps.

"You aren't getting between Chris and I."

"Has a girl ever gotten between you two?"

"Once or twice, but we vowed to not let one do so again." Alex says as we climb onto the empty elevator.

"Don't you guys get offended when the other tells you that they don't like the girl?" I ask curiously as he pushes the four button.

"It does hurt, we do get offended as most people would. Sometimes we don't listen because we are both stubborn."

"How do you realize to break up with the girl if you can't trust your own best friend? I mean, that must be a lot of apologies." I said.

"We do eventually break up with the girl or else I wouldn't be on this 'singles' cruise." He said doing air quotes around singles.

"Ha ha." I say as we climb off the elevator heading to our

rooms.

"Any previous boyfriends I should know about?" Alex asked.

"None that are worth my breath." I say not wanting to bring up my ex and how broken he left me.

"I should be relieved about that, huh?"

"I would be." I say as we step in front of my door.

"Good night, Tara." Alex says as he leans forward wrapping his arms around me in a big hug and I slowly wrap mine around his body giving him one back. I oddly really wanted a good night kiss instead; a hug would do the job though.

"Night, Alex." I say smiling as I let myself into my room forgetting I still have his jacket.

Chapter Fourteen:

After hanging up Alex's jacket, I changed back into my pajamas. I plug my phone in before I climb into the bed. I hoped to get a long night of sleep, but that didn't play out according to plan. I am woken up by loud knocking at the door, I grumpily reach over smacking around for my phone. Once my hand lands on my phone, my hand grips it and brings it to my face. I read 0230 as the time. Another knock comes to the door, who is knocking on my door this early?

"God dang it." I say as I sit up rubbing my eyes. I run my hand through my hair as I head to the connecting door, opening it to a very wide-awake Alex, "What?"

"Were you asleep?" Alex asked.

"No...like normal people, I like to exercise at 2:30 AM." I say sarcastically as I yawn.

"You want to go get some coffee?" Alex asks.

"I'll need some to get through this day." I walk back into my room, Alex follows me in. I begin to pull my sweats on over the shorts I have on. "I hung your jacket up." I said nodding towards the closet cove.

"I totally forgot about it." Alex says as he reaches for his jacket. While he was there, Alex picked up my purse and retrieved my phone from the nightstand. Alex turns around to hand the two items to me.

"You didn't see my wallpaper, did you?" I asked nervously knowing that my wallpaper is a picture of Xavier and me.

"No, why? Am I in it?" Alex asked with a cocky smile.

"No." I say as I pull my purse onto my shoulder and lead him out of my room, "Is anything open?"

"We'll find out."

"Why are you up at this time?" I asked curiously.

"I was a restless sleeper again; I was thinking too much."

"About what?" I asked curiously. This time I push the down button on the elevator panel.

"It's nothing." He said with a shrug.

"It's something if you are having a hard time sleeping."

"It's stupid." Alex says but I can tell that whatever is keeping him awake is really bothering him. We climb onto the elevator shaft that is going to take us down to the main floor.

"You know, I never expected to be getting coffee at 2:30 in the morning when I agreed to go on this cruise."

"But you never expected to meet me either." Alex notes as we climb off the elevator.

"Do you always have long nights?" I ask as I let him lead us to a coffee shop.

"It depends on if we are traveling." Alex says as he pulls the glass door open.

"How many hours do you guys travel at night?" I ask curiously as I look around the empty shop.

"Not that many. Don't you ever work night shifts?"

"Yep. I'm normally on the clock for eighteen plus hours."

"Really? Eighteen hours?" Alex asks as I look over the choices of coffee to get.

"Yeah, they usually try to give me the next day off but sometimes that doesn't happen." I shrug. Alex steps up to the counter to order his drink.

"I'll have a Cafe Americano with four shots and whatever she wants." Alex says, pointing back at me.

"Alex, you don't have to."

"It's my pleasure, especially since I woke you up this early." Alex reassures me.

"I'll have the same."

"Do you even like Café Americano?"

"I'll find out." I said smiling.

"Make that a Vanilla Latte with four shots." Alex says to the barista, he turns to me and says, "This time I'll let you try it."

"Promise promises." I said snickering.

"Shut up." Alex said teasingly.

"Until you prove it, I will just keep thinking you're making promises you won't keep." I say smiling as he pays the bill. We stand aside watching them make our drinks.

"How many of these do you drink during a normal shift?"

"Surprisingly, I usually drink two coffees and two five-hour energies."

"What does your job need you to do for eighteen hours?" Alex asks confused when he is handed his drink.

"My regular shifts aren't supposed to be that long but on top of dealing with all the medical emergencies that take place and having to do all the paperwork, meetings, briefings among everything else I am always stuck there for eighteen hours minimum." I say as he hands me his drink after he takes a sip,

I stare at it for a moment.

"I don't have cooties and I didn't lick it too much."

"Do you lick your lids often?"

"Not that often, lids aren't that tasty...are you going to take a sip?" Alex asked.

"Absolutely." I grab his drink and take a sip. Alex seems shocked that I did it. "Why do you seem so shocked?"

"You're the first girl that would do that."

"I like being treated like one of the guys." I say handing the drink back to him.

"If you only had a sister, why do you want to be treated like one of the guys?" Alex asked as I handed him the drink and we walk the short distance to a table. Alex pulls my chair out for me, and he sits down across from me.

"I've always acted like one of the guys. My dad left my sister and I at a young age, I kind of became a tom boy. I guess I wanted to be the male role model in my sister's life."

"I would have loved to hear you do the birds and bees conversation as a male figure."

"I didn't have that conversation...it was the reason I never dated until later in life."

"When was the last official date you went on?" Alex asks as he is holding his cup in his lap looking at me intently.

"Quite a few years ago." I say honestly.

"And that was when?" Alex said. I shift in my seat, trying not to get emotional or uncomfortable talking about what happened.

"2017." I say softly.

"Did you just say 2017?" He asks. His mouth falls open when it clicks how long it truly has been since I had gone out with anyone.

"Yeah, the breakup was hard. We were engaged and he called it off." I say, downing some coffee like it is a shot.

"How old are you?"

"Not as old as I look." I say chuckling.

"We all look older than we are, it's called aging." Alex says.

"Amen."

"You never answered me." Alex replies.

"I was born in 1990."

"89, not much of a difference and why do I look older than you?" Alex asks.

"I don't have a five o'clock shadow and I have make-up to help enhance my appearance when I want it to."

"I can wear make-up too?" Alex asks.

"I never liked a man that would wear more makeup than I do."

"Are you saying you like me?"

"I just said I don't like men that wear more makeup than I do, there are a lot of men that fit that."

"Have you met a man that wears more than you?"

"Surprisingly, yes." I answer.

"Are you sure they weren't drag queens or a clown?"

"They didn't look like drag queens." I say before we drop quiet for a moment.

"What kind of kid were you? Straight A student or a slacker?" Alex asks.

"A mixture of both, I never went below a C in any of my classes. I was on the soccer team and was kind of a loner." I said trying to remember my high school days.

"Aw, you were one of those." Alex said, nodding.

"Who were you?"

"I was totally a slacker. I skipped a lot of classes and would rather be skating. Now that I'm older, I realized how stupid that was."

"What made you realize that it was stupid?" I ask curiously.

"I missed a lot of my education and moments I'll never get back. I just keep thinking of what my kids will think when they find out how much I missed, and they can use that against me."

"I feel you. Never once do you think about that when you're in high school. Now that we're older, we really reflect on our bad judgments that were made back in the day."

"Exactly. My parents threaten me with the 'wait until you have a kid like you' and I can just imagine. Did you ever get that?"

"Yeah, a few times." I say smiling. I like that our conversation was reminiscing our younger days, "Did you go to prom?"

"Yes, but man did I wish I didn't. That was filled with drama, I don't like drama."

"Mine wasn't the only one drama filled then. I didn't even want to go."

"I didn't want to go either. It seemed so dumb, but my parents insisted that I go."

"Mine too. It was like any other dance, but you got dinner."

"Exactly. Now I have to go to an event similar to that every year." Alex said.

"Really?"

"We either have a holiday party or a ball before our biggest Pay-Per-View. We all go, and we bring our families for a little get together."

"Do you go to them?" I ask, he sighs. Alex runs a hand through his hair as if he is trying to think of a way to answer that.

"There are very few of us that have a lucky person in their lives. There are people like me that aren't that fortunate and it's hard going to these events with all these happy families. It rubs it in my face that I haven't found the one or haven't started my own family."

"I see how it can be painful, it's like a constant reminder." I nod my head in understanding.

"Have you ever had that?"

"Much so. Life is too short and I'm afraid that my life will be cut off too short before I find that person."

"We all have a fear of dying alone."

Awkward silence comes over our table. "Alexander." I say, twisting the coffee cup in my hand. I need to tell him. He has to know I have a son. If I want a relationship with him, I want it to be an honest one. I don't want to lie to him.

I'm not sure what came over me. Maybe it's the caffeine. Maybe because we are having these open conversations with each other. Or that I'm so tired from being woken up at two in the morning. I got a random burst of confidence. His ears are perked intrigued in what I am going to say next.

"Whoa, full name. Must be serious if you are going with my full name." I glare up at him, not enthused at all. He takes a long sip of his coffee staring back at me intensely waiting for me to speak.

"I have a son."

There I said it! He knows and it's out in the open. There is no more hiding. His expression doesn't change at all, he doesn't seem at all shocked. "A son?"

"Yes. His name is Xavier and he's six. He'll be seven in February."

"That's not a problem. I'm a kid too sometimes."

"You don't care that I have a son?"

"No, why would I?" He asks, confused. I shrug my shoulders while taking a drink from my coffee.

"My ex called our engagement off because I adopted Xavier."

"Adopted?" Alex asks, I sigh knowing I need to tell him the whole truth.

"Yes, he's my sister's son. She was with an abusive guy; she ran when she got pregnant with his kid. Come delivery, she didn't make it. Beforehand, she had me vow that I'll take him. She did not want him to go into the system or worse, the dad. I went through months of paperwork, court hearings and interviews to get him to be mine. Then my ex broke it off, he didn't understand why I agreed to be a mom to a kid that wasn't even mine." I explain. I stare blankly at the table. I can't believe I spilled the whole truth to Alex.

Now it was all out in the open, Alex was for sure going to call it quits. I wasn't going to stick around to hear him tell me, it was best just for me to leave. Panicking internally that I had just been honest and open with him. I jump to my feet and grab my coffee. "I'm going back to my room to get some sleep."

I make a beeline out of the coffee shop, not waiting up for Alex at all and hurry back to my room. I let myself in and dive onto the firm single mattress with the dark blue comforter that did a poor job at keeping me warm. I curl into the fetal position. I can't believe I just did that. I fight back tears; I am so upset that I just destroyed this relationship, just like the last one for doing what was right.

Chapter Fifteen:

Alex's Point of View-

I turn in my seat as my eyes follow Tara out of the coffee shop, not sure why she rushed out of here in a panic. I look back to the counter where the two female employees stared at me with judgmental looks. They probably thought I had said something to cause Tara to react like that.

I stand up taking my coffee with me, I feel myself moving slowly. *Tara was a mom. She has been a mom for six years, no wonder why she hasn't dated. She never had the time.* I think to myself as I drift to the railing to look out over the ocean. *No wonder she got upset when I was asking about her taking more time off. She couldn't because she has a kid to provide for. Her ex left her to be the struggling single mom that she is. Tara is probably afraid to love again thinking she will get hurt. She was engaged to that idiot. Who would leave the woman they loved so much over a kid? I loved kids. Would I want to be a dad to Xavier? Am I ready? Would he even like me? What if the kid doesn't even like me?*

I sigh and run a hand through my hair, thoughts racing

through my head. I turn around, leaning back against the railing not wanting to look at the ocean. The view isn't helping at all to clear my mind. I head back into the mall of shops, taking my time to look over the window displays of every shop.

I'm not only going to be dating Tara, but I am also going to be dating her son. I have to win him over too. I think as I step in front of the window with a bunch of souvenirs displayed in it. My eyes looking over what they have to offer, I think this will be the best shop to look at. I pull open the door, fortunately it is open at this hour. I walk leisurely through the store letting my gaze browse over all the various shelves until I get to the kid's section.

I stop in front of that shelf, my eyes browsing over what is being sold. *What would a six-year-old boy like? Legos? Superheroes?* I ponder as I pick up different toys, setting them each back down until I decide on a Lego set that builds the Batmobile. I purchase the toy before I make my way back up to Tara's room hoping that she has calmed down enough from whatever it was to talk with me.

I stand in front of her door; I raise my hand to knock and can't find the strength to hit the fist against the hideous colored door. I look at the toy in the white plastic bag then to the door. *Did I like this woman enough to become a stepdad? Was I ready to take on the dad role? I always wanted to be a dad. What if Tara doesn't want more kids? Would I be ok with just having Xavier as my only child?*

The door bangs open before I can even knock once, I gasp from being startled and step back a little.

"Hey." She says softly.

"Hey." I reply back. I lift the plastic bag that holds the Lego set, "I bought Xavier a toy, do you think he'll like it?"

Tara's lips curl up into a smile, her face lights up with happiness.

"He'll love it, Alex. May we talk though?"

"I think we should." I say in a more serious tone. "You want to go get breakfast? I would suggest coffee, but I'm caffeinated out."

"Ok." She agrees. I hand her the plastic bag; I hold the door open watching as she puts the toy on top of her suitcase. We both step out into the open hallway. I lead her down to a bagel place I had passed earlier when I was trying to clear my mind. The whole walk is in awkward silence. Tara slides into a black garden type table that is seated for two while I order our breakfast. I return to our table with two brown paper bags that hold the Everything Bagels I ordered us.

"Everything bagel with cream cheese." I state handing her one of the bags. I rip the bag to use as the plate for my bagel. I pull out the freshly made pastry and the small white container of cream cheese. Without looking up at her, "You have a six-year-old son?"

"Yes. Look, be honest with me Alex-" She begins to say, I glance up at her from watching the cream cheese being spread onto half the bagel, "Is there any chance? I'm not going to continue whatever this is between us, getting my hopes further up that there is something going to come out of it only to be turned down."

"And why would I turn this down if it was to happen?" I ask, I toss the plastic knife down in agitation. I lean back in the black metal seat, upset that she would even think I am the type of person that would turn this down. I really like her, and I wasn't bothered by her having a son.

155

"Because I have a son."

"Because you have a son, you think I'll turn love down?" I ask curiously. Tara looks at me confused, "You haven't dated much since you adopted him?"

"No, I haven't. Who would want to date a single mom?" She asks, she looks down into her lap.

"I'm not that type. I love kids and would love to know more about Xavier. If he is your son, then he will be my son too. I'm not like most guys and not all guys are jerks like your ex. I really like you, Tara. I may be upset that you withheld this information from me, happy you told me before I found out the hard way but I'm not the other type of guy."

"What type of guy is that?"

"The type of guy that won't date a beautiful woman because she's a single mom. Maybe I'm crazy over one. I know that you are the type of girl that works harder than anyone I've ever known. I was hoping that the same girl would give this rock star of a wrestler a chance. Consider this plan, that this weekend you have no kid. I want you to live your life and let whatever happens happen." I say. I bite into my bagel, setting the bagel back down and dust the crumbs off my hands.

"What about after the boat?"

"We'll worry about that when the cruise docks." I say confidently, "By then, we will know where we stand with each other."

"You still want to know me?"

"Of course. But right now, if we do get serious, I want to know about this Xavier kid. I need to know how to win his heart so he can like me." I say truthfully. Tara busts out into laughter. "What? If we're going to be serious, he needs to like me too if I'm going to be his stepdad."

"Speaking of which, I would want whoever I marry to adopt him. Would you sign the paperwork to legally adopt him?"

"In a heartbeat. I always wanted to be a dad. Would you want to have your own kids? I would like us to have more kids." I say truthfully. She smiles and pushes a strand of hair behind her ear. I think that she was so scared that I would run, and she would lose the one guy that seemed interested in her in years. The heartbreak she must have gone through because of her ex, they had to have been madly in love if they were going to get married.

"I would love to have more kids of my own. I have sheltered myself from finding mister right, so I gave up hope of having my own or even finding my true love until-"

"Until I walked in." I say with a cocky smile, she laughs and smiles too.

"Until you walked in. Absolutely. It rekindled these feelings I had that I haven't felt in years. I got scared because I thought about my ex and the hurt I endured when he left me because of Xavier. I love my son so much, I closed myself off not wanting to get hurt again. It isn't just me anymore that will get hurt, I have a son who is going to have to go through the same thing."

"I totally understand." I say, nodding my head.

"Anyways, Xavier loves dinosaurs and Batman. He wants to be Batman for Halloween next month; he's roped me into being Harley Quinn. He said he needs a bad guy to chase."

"But you aren't that bad." I say with a chuckle, "You said that he is your sister's kid?" I ask and she nods her head yes as she rips the pastry bag open. "She got pregnant by an abusive guy?"

"Yep, she ran and never looked back when she got pregnant. I vowed to protect him from that moron."

"Has he ever tried to make contact with Xavier?" I ask crossing my arms over my chest becoming very protective and worrisome about their safety.

Tara sighed, "Only once, but nothing since."

Just hearing that he has tried one time made me worried about her and Xavier, "Xavier and you are always safe with Chris and me. Do you have an alarm system at your house?"

"I do have a security system that my mom and I both know the codes to. Xavier's school and daycare are aware of the situation unfortunately because I do not want the guy thinking to show up there. I have already switched daycares four times." Tara explains, I hate that she had to endure this and try to protect the boy from the abuser.

"Would you consider moving out of state?" I ask, she lifts her glare to look up at me. Our eyes connect; she is confused as to what I am getting at.

"What are you getting at Alex?"

"I have a house in Grand Rapids, there are MGM resorts down in Detroit. It might be a couple hour drive from Grand Rapids but maybe you can request a transfer. The abuser won't find you there." I say taking another bite of my bagel.

"I'll have to think long and hard about that Alex." She says. I watch her break a piece of the bagel off to give a taste. Her face contorts in disgust, and I burst into laughter at the face she just made.

"You don't like it?"

"Not really. Never tried it before." She responds truthfully.

"You want a muffin instead?" I offer. Tara nods her head yes. I get up from the table walking the short distance to the front counter ordering some juice and a fresh blueberry muffin for Tara. I turn to look at her with a smile on my face. I pull out the black leather wallet that I have tucked in my butt pocket and hooked to my pants by a silver chain. After paying for the new order, I walk back to the table and slide back into my seat to wait until the muffin is zapped. "Why do I feel like you are the Pinterest mom."

"Ha! Do you know how much I work? I barely have time to spend with my son, much less any projects. I got McDonald's on speed dial for delivery. Peanut butter and jelly are a common dinner."

"Nothing wrong with the classic Golden Arches or peanut butter and jelly. I'm more of a cereal man."

"You can eat cereal on your diet?"

"Yes, I can. Cereal has a lot more vitamins than you think and add in the milk."

"How do you know?"

"Certified nutritionist." I say taking another bite of my bagel, "Why do you think I diet?"

"Your career."

"I can eat well and still have these abs."

"You got abs?" She asks with a chuckle. I give her a glare.

"I thought you got a very nice view of my upper body when I gave you that strip tease. You keep wanting more. I'm starting to think you just want me because I'm eye candy." I say pushing a hand through my hair.

"Oh yes Alex, pure eye candy." She says with a roll of her eyes. My phone chimes at the same time that my name is being called at the counter, "I'll get the muffin if you want to take that call."

I answer my phone listening to my boss ramble on about certain coworkers' schedules, not fully paying attention. I watch Tara walking up to the dark chestnut wood counter to pick up the order. My eyes landing on her behind as she walks, *DON'T LOOK THERE YOU PERVERT!* I yell at myself. I am attracted to her, the long auburn hair, her bright smile, purest heart around, and those blue eyes of hers. It is like I am staring into crystals. I feel myself falling in love with her.

"Uh-huh, I'll do it. See you then." I hang up the call.

"What was that about?" She asks while I sit my phone on the table.

"I have to fill in for some events today, would love for you to tag along."

"You sure?" She asks with uncertainty in her voice.

"I would rather you accompany me than Chris. I can only stand so much of that Gumby." I say with a soft chuckle, she lets out a laugh too. "When will I be meeting mom and Xavier?"

"When I feel it's time."

"What about Halloween? I can go trick or treating with you guys, added security."

"Only if you promise to be my Joker." She says with a laugh.

"Well duh. You can't have a Harley Quinn without a Joker." I say seriously. She laughs again, "You don't think I will do it, do you?"

"I don't think you will, that is your ultimate test. If you are truly cut out for it, you'll be willing to dress up for Halloween and make an idiot out of yourself."

"I am SO doing it. You obviously don't know who I am."

"We will see if you uphold this promise." She says with a bright smile, and I smile too. She has no idea that I am totally going along with this. I am going to go full force, I want this to work so bad. "When do you have to be at these things you are having to fill in at?"

"Two. Do you want some actual food? I was thinking of

going back up to the rooms, ordering room service and binge watching something."

"Sounds great, we both need rest after the long night we had." She says as we begin to clean up our table. I lead her back to our rooms, I let her unlock her room and we step in. I watch her kick her shoes off before she belly flops onto the bed. I know it had to have hurt because these beds are on the firmer side of mattresses.

"Is there room for me?" I ask as she rolls over to give me room. I slide onto the bed, laying on my side and slide my arm under her head. I close my eyes trying to just rest them for a little bit before I have to order some real food and get ready for my obligations.

Chapter Sixteen:

Tara's Point Of View-

I lay on my side, I feel dead to the world from how exhausted I am. I hear the loud beats of that rock song Alex has set for his ringtone. My eyes flutter open, now staring at the soft features of Alex's face. He is still asleep. I gently shake him to try to wake him up, but he won't budge. I groan as I sit up and try to think of how I can get to his phone. I try to reach over him and can't reach his phone. I then begin to climb over him, straddling his lap when I hear a moan. His eyes flutter open, and our eyes connect.

"What are you doing? If you are going to grope me, at least wake me up so I can enjoy it."

"I'm not groping you, Alex." I said in a proper tone.

"Then tell me why I woke up to a beautiful lady like yourself straddling my waist?"

"I was trying to turn off that horrid ringtone of yours."

"You don't have to lie to me in order to grope me." He laughs as he reaches for his phone and turns it off. I fall back onto the bed beside him.

"Why do you automatically assume I want to grope you?"

"Who doesn't?" Alex asks cockily. I roll my eyes as I begin to crawl off the bed a different way when I hear my phone ringing now, Alex looks at it and begins laughing as he picks it up, "Thank you for calling Mr. Sexy-rooni's Pizza Parlor, may I take your order? She's right here…tonight's game night…will you be able to play?…oh she is going…"

"I am?" I ask as I lean against the wall. Alex nods as I assume he is listening to Chris on the other end of the phone.

"We will, bye Chris." Alex says as he hangs up, "Us three are going to game night."

"You want to explore the rest of the boat?" I ask.

"Absolutely." Alex says, "But first food, I thought we were going to order room service?"

"We were but I think we both zonked out from exhaustion before we even ordered food."

"Sounds like us, you want to order some now? I would like to shower up before we leave the room." I ask.

"Sure, breakfast?"

"Cereal?" I respond as he smiles wide.

"You know it." He says as he climbs off my bed to go into his own room. The door that connects our two rooms has probably stayed open for most of this trip. I grab a new outfit for the day then walk into the bathroom to freshen myself up and wake up more from the rough night we had.

I am just so relieved that Alex knows about Xavier, so I don't have to continue lying or withholding information from him. I get dressed and do everything that I need to do in the bathroom before I head back into the main bedroom.

I walk out to the main room seeing that Alex is back in my

bed, laying on his back with his head propped up on his hands. He is wearing black boots, a pair of light blue denim jeans, the silver chain dangling from it again, a black shirt with the Red-Hot Chili Peppers logo and his leather jacket. He always has that look to him, but I find it attractive. I walk over to my suitcase pushing my dirty clothes into it before he can see them.

"Is that a dinosaur?" Alex asks.

"Oh, yeah. I bought it for Xavier." I answer.

"How many dinosaurs does he have?" Alex asks when a knock comes from his room, "Our cereal awaits." He jumps out of the bed and makes a dash for his door. I have to laugh, there is no getting between him and that cereal. He returns with the tray that has two bowls on it.

"Thanks, Alex. Fruity Pebbles?" I ask, finally taking notice of what kind of cereal it is.

"Uh, yeah! They are the best." Alex says, I smile and roll my eyes. He is a giant kid, and he will get along great with Xavier. Alex sits on the edge of my bed holding the bowl in his lap. He reaches for the remote, flicking the television on and begins to surf through the different channels.

"Why does the ship not have any good channels?" Alex asks before he turns the television back off after not finding anything he wants to watch.

"We're on a boat in the middle of the ocean. It's not like we can get cable." I say as I slide my shoes on.

"What about Dish network or something?"

"That's still a lot of boxes and cables. I don't know if they'll get signal." I say. Now that we don't have the distraction of the television, we are able to eat our cereal faster. "I'm intrigued to find out."

Chapter Sixteen:

"Test it." I say.

"I may." Alex says as we head out of the room.

"How would you test it unless you own your own cruise ship?"

"Then I'll buy a cruise ship. Well, maybe not a cruise ship because those things are expensive so maybe a smaller boat."

"You can't go too small." I say.

"But if I buy one, I can take you sailing again to help cure your boat fear." Alex says as he smirks at me.

"I don't think so. I don't trust you as a captain of a boat."

"Why not?" Alex asks as I push the down button for the elevator.

"You don't even know how to operate a boat." I say.

"How do you know that?"

"Then prove it. Let's go to the captain's deck and see if we can steer the boat."

"Let's do that."

"I wonder if they'll even let us steer it." I say as we both climb onto the elevator going down to the main floor.

"I don't see why they won't, at least stand next to us in case we royally screw up."

"Especially with you. You'll be worse than me."

"No, I won't." Alex says.

"We'll find out. Do you know where it's at?" I ask as we climb off the elevator.

"We'll find it soon enough. I think it's this way." Alex says as he points to the side of the boat that I haven't been this whole trip.

"I think it's up." I say jokingly.

"That's where the rooms are so I think we need to either go further up or a different way."

"Wouldn't that crew member know?" I nod to the man who is obviously a crew member.

"You know men don't ask for directions."

"Fine, I'll go ask." I say leaving Alex's side approaching the crew member stopping him momentarily, "Sorry to bother you but how do you get to the captain's deck?"

"I was heading there now; would you like me to show you?" He asks.

"Please." I say before waving Alex to come. Alex groans before he catches up to us. "Thanks."

"No problem, ma'am." The employee says.

"Ooohhh, you got called ma'am." Alex says, looking at me.

"Shut up, Alex."

"Do you think that we'll be able to steer the ship?" Alex asks as we join the employee on the elevator.

"Yes sir, you will be able to steer the ship momentarily."

"Momentarily means a few seconds, not a whole trip." I say looking at Alex.

"I bet I can still drive it better than you." Alex says.

"It's more like a car, no one is better than another." The employee says.

"See?" I say, trying to prove my point.

"We'll see." Alex says as we climb off the elevator following close behind the employee. Alex grabs my hand, his hand cups mine. I look down at our connecting hands then up to Alex who is blushing a little, "I don't want to lose you."

"If you want to hold my hand, all you have to do is ask." I say when we make eye contact again.

"Okay." Alex says as we begin heading after the employee. I start to run but Alex doesn't, the connection of our hands pulls me back to look at him.

"Come on." I say as I am trying to pull him to catch up to the employee.

"We aren't in any rush." Alex says as I roll my eyes. We walk at his pace to the open door that leads into the captain's deck. We see men in uniform filling the room and each crew member doing a different task than the other.

"Good afternoon, I'm Captain Harry." The Captain walks up to us and shakes our hands.

"That's some sight." I say looking out the large windows that fill the front of the room. I walk up to stand beside the person that is driving at the moment. I feel Alex's presence behind me along with a hand resting on my hip. I look over my shoulder seeing him and smile before I look back out the window.

"Was that a whale?" Alex asks, pointing out to a big water commotion ahead.

"Yep, you will see a lot of whales and dolphins in this area. Would you like to steer the ship?" Harry asks.

"May we?" I ask turning to look at the Captain.

"Absolutely." Harry says as I slide between Alex and a crew member to meet the Captain at the wheel. "Keep it as still as possible." Harry instructs as I put my hands on the wheel holding it still.

"This is awesome. Alex, could you take a picture?" I ask Alex.

"Where is your phone?" Alex asks as I pull it out of my pocket with one hand before I quickly put it back on the wheel. Alex grabs my phone from me to take a picture of me steering the boat.

"You want to drive?" I ask Alex with a smile.

"Well, duh!" Alex says as he hands me my phone back and he takes control of the wheel. I snap a photo of him. "I want a copy of that."

"You will get one." I say as I text the photo to Alex before I forget. I put my phone back into my pocket before I look back out to the ocean view in front of the room.

"You want another go?" Alex asks as I look at him smiling.

"Yeah." I say as I grab the wheel trying to hold it as still as I can. I look out into the beautiful ocean. I don't notice Alex taking photos with his phone and handing it off to a crew member. Alex steps close behind me putting his hands on top of mine.

"Are you okay?" Alex whispers into my left ear. I turn to that side to look at him and I can see the concerned look in his eyes.

"Yeah, it's just so beautiful. Look at all those dolphins. I just feel so free up here." I say as I look back at the ocean ahead of us.

"You're more beautiful." I hear Alex whisper right outside my ear.

"Thanks, sir. I think we are going to explore more of the boat." I say as I step out from in front of Alex.

"You're very welcome." Harry says. Alex grabs my hand as we head out of the room after he got his phone back from the crew member.

"How was that?" Alex asks as we walk out of the room.

"I loved it. I wonder if they have a viewing deck to look out of." I say, wanting to try to see more whales and dolphins.

"You want to whale watch more, don't you?" Alex asks as we head back down the hall that we came down earlier.

"I've always wanted to but never got around to it. Maybe that's why I want to watch more." I say walking slower and he slows down as well. We begin swinging our hands between us.

"I'll take you whale watching." Alex says.

"That'll be fun. I'll be more worried that I'll have worse sea sickness."

"Not if you take your medicine like a patient instead of a nurse."

"Have you been?"

"Once in seventh grade, well it wasn't really whale watching though." Alex says as we get to the elevators.

"What was the trip then?" I ask.

"We all went ice fishing. It sucked because we couldn't go onto Mackinaw Island until everyone had caught one fish."

"How many people were in your class?" I ask as the elevator tings as the doors open. He climbs onto the elevator; I push the right button before Alex pulls me to stand in front of him as he leans back against the railing.

"That went…um…I want to say at least a hundred of us." Alex says.

"Where did you put that many fish? And if you were ice fishing, were you even able to take a boat?"

"We used a boat; it wasn't completely iced over, and I don't exactly remember where our fish went. That was when I was in seventh grade, and I could care less about the fish."

"Who would want that many fish? I don't even eat that much fish in a lifetime."

"What kind of fish do you eat?" Alex asks.

"Fish sticks and tuna fish." I say as the elevator doors open, and we walk off.

"No sushi?"

"I can barely stand the taste of tuna without overusing the mayo." I say as I let him lead the way. Our hands are still connected which I didn't mind, I actually enjoy it.

"I guess I'm just used to fish due to living in Michigan."

"I should be used to it since I have lived in Vegas my whole life and we offer sushi at the buffet on the daily, but I get grossed out." I say with a disgusted face.

"Very true, fish is very different from anything else. It is very much an acquired taste."

"To each their own." I shrug when we find the pool.

"They had a pool this whole time." Alex says as we stand at the entrance to the room with the pool.

"I've never been on a cruise ship before, but I think every one has a pool." I say.

"You want to dip your feet in?"

"Why not?" I ask as we walk to the edge rolling our pant legs up. I take my socks and shoes off and put my phone in my purse, putting them far from the edge. We both slowly sit down putting our feet into the water. "I should push you into the water to make up for pushing Chris in."

"You know what would happen if you did that?" Alex asks as I look up at him from staring at my feet that are swaying in the water below.

"What?" I ask curiously.

"You're going in with me."

"You won't do that." I say.

"Try it."

"I will." I say as I push him in. Alex grabs my hand pulling me with him to get us both to fall under the water laughing at each other when we resurface.

"Told you!" Alex says while we are kicking our feet to stay afloat in the deep end.

"You did. It was worth a shot." I say smiling as I go to reach for the side, and he grabs my waist pulling me back.

"Where do you think you're going?" Alex asks, holding me

back far enough so I can't grab the edge. I begin kicking and trying to pry his arms off me.

"Let me go!" I say laughing as he tosses me towards the shallow end. I resurface spitting out water and pushing hair out of my face, "Thanks for that."

"Sh!" He says, reaching out, putting a finger to my lips to make me go quiet. I look at him as I am trying to listen to what he is trying to hear. I hear footsteps and chatter. "Someone is coming, duck."

"Why? Are you scared of being seen?" I say.

"No, but I know that voice and I don't want to get in trouble."

"Who is it?" I asked, smiling.

"My boss." Alex says.

"Great, does that mean I can tell him that I am having issues with you and that you just ruined my whole outfit?" I ask and try to tease him. He rolls his eyes pushing me down with him, holding my breath as much as I can. Alex and I are making faces trying to stay hidden until we don't hear them anymore.

I point up to symbolize that I am going up; I resurface and don't hear or see anyone. I look over at Alex waving to signal that the coast is clear. I pull myself out of the water and sit on the edge of the pool.

"I guess now will be the time to head back to our rooms." I say looking down into Alex's hazel eyes. Alex places his arms on the edge of the pool and rests his chin on his arms.

"Why? We still have time to spare, don't we?" Alex says.

"Yeah, but we are both soaked head to toe. I don't see us being allowed to do much like this."

"You may be wrong." Alex says as he pulls himself up plopping down beside me.

"I'm never wrong." I say jokingly.

"I'm sure you are at some point."

"Like I was wrong about you." I say as I get up heading to my socks and shoes. I pull my socks out of where I stuffed them in my shoes before I put them on. I begin sliding my shoes on and reach for my purse. I pull my phone out to check for any notifications before sliding it back into my purse. I look over to Alex who is still sitting there, and he looks like he is deep in thought about something.

"How were you wrong about me?" Alex asks finally, he doesn't even turn around.

"When we first met, I wasn't sure how this weekend would be and thought I would have an annoying neighbor. You proved me wrong."

"In a good way, right?" Alex asks, looking over his shoulder at me.

"Oh no, it's totally in a bad way." I say sarcastically. Alex jumps up from where he was sitting running towards me, "No running near the pool!" I exclaim as he chases me out of the pool room.

"Ow! I just stubbed my toe." Alex says, jumping on his one foot as we turn a corner.

"That's what you get for running near the pool." I say with a laugh. He gives me a glare before I follow him back into the pool area so he can put his socks and shoes back on. He grabs my hand as we walk back out of the pool area and get weird looks from everyone.

"Why is everyone looking at us?"

"I don't know. It could be that we are dripping wet for no apparent reason." I say sarcastically. Alex and I head up to our room trying so hard not to drip water as much as we can. We try not to walk on the tiled flooring to avoid slipping but the challenge will be getting to the fourth floor without having to walk on portions of tile flooring.

We got to a part of the ship that is strictly tiled flooring, we hold onto each other as we are slipping on the water that is dripping from our bodies. We can't help but to laugh as we are slipping and sliding. We get to the elevators, pushing the up button, and use the wall for support while we wait. We climb onto the elevator that is carpeted to head up to the fourth floor. I look over to see Alex wringing out his shirt by twisting a piece of the hem and I just giggle. He looks up at me with his bright smile.

"What? I'm just helping it dry." Alex says with a shrug.

"Nothing, won't you get in trouble?"

"Why would I get in trouble?" Alex asks as I nod up to the mini ball in the corner of the elevator shaft that is obviously a security camera, "Psh, what are the odds that they will be able to find me in one night? We dock tomorrow afternoon and where are they going to kick me off at? We are in the middle of the ocean."

"Very true, but I don't need you to be put in cruise jail for the remainder of the trip."

"Why do you care?" Alex asks, I know he is just egging me on to say that I like him.

"I don't care. I just don't want you to ruin the rest of the trip." I say blushing some.

"If this is the one thing that gets me in trouble, then I haven't been as bad as I thought I was." Alex says as the elevator doors dings before opening. We climb off the elevator, and he reaches over to grasp my hand, "What do you have planned for the rest of the day?"

"I have to go do the Family Feud game at two, you want to

come?"

"How does that work?"

"I'll explain later, are you coming?" He asks as he tugs my arm to turn to look at him. We stand facing each other in front of my room.

"I think I can, if it means I'll spend more time with you." I say sheepishly.

"It does, go get changed and we'll go together." He says with a smile.

"We still have an hour and a half though."

"I know, women take a while to get ready from what I'm told." He says with a wink before he pushes his door open and disappears inside.

Chapter Seventeen:

Alex walks through the threshold that connects our rooms carrying the whole phone receiver, the pale pink phone pressed to his ear. I sit up straight from being bent over from tying my shoes.

"Do you mind?" I ask.

"No, not at all. You want something from room service?" He asks as he moves the phone away from his mouth.

"What about Family Feud?"

"We have just enough time for room service, don't you worry."

"I'll have a cheeseburger." I say. I know it is something simple and that majority of room services would have it. He nods as he walks back into his room. I climb onto my bed scooting as close as I can to the wall and flip the television on. I begin to flip through channels until I find Criminal Minds.

"It'll be about a half hour until they can get it up to us." Alex says as he enters the room and leaves that door open. I assume so we can hear the knock when the food arrives. Alex climbs onto the bed beside me getting comfortable and wraps his arm around me.

"How does that Family Feud work? I understand what Family Feud is but how does it work with you guys?"

"Five of us stars compete against five lucky fans that get chosen. We have to answer questions about the wrestling promotion or the wrestlers of the promotion."

"I assume that the stars would win, but then again you are on their team." I say as his arm hangs over my shoulder.

"I can be smart."

"Can be is the key term in that sentence."

"I just choose not to be. Life is too short not to have fun."

"Nothing is wrong with having fun." I say, smiling as I look over making eye contact with his beautiful eyes.

"How often do you have fun?"

"Everyday."

"Why do I not believe you?" Alex asks, giving me a questionable look.

"Because you know I'm lying and know that I'm nothing but a workaholic."

"Has this weekend at least been fun?"

"Nope, someone by the name of Alex has ruined it." I say smiling as he climbs on top of me tickling me in the spot he accidentally found.

"Really? You're laughing now. Are you having fun yet?" Alex asks.

"No!" I exclaim while kicking trying to get him off of me.

"I'm not going to stop tickling you until you say that you're having fun." Alex says. I am trying to pull his arms away from my body, but he is getting in random tickles.

"I'm having fun!" I exclaim as he smiles his wicked smile,

"What is with that smile?"

"You're truly having fun hanging with me, aren't you?" Alex asks while his facial features lighten from happiness.

"Not as much as you are."

"Who said that I was?"

"You implied it." I say when a knock comes from his room. We know that it must be room service.

"Lunch." Alex says climbing off my lap and starts to climb the rest of the way off the bed.

"No, that's the door." I say jokingly. Alex gives me a dirty look and I give him a joking smile.

Alex walks over to his room to answer his door and gets lunch for us. I maneuver myself to where there will be room to sit my plate in front of me. Alex comes into the room carrying a brown tray that has two plates with silver lids covering them.

He rests the tray on the dresser then picks up the plates.

"Cheeseburger for you and cheeseburger for me." Alex sets one plate in front of me and the other in front of where he will sit, "I'm going to go down to the vending machines to buy a drink, you want a drink?"

"Where are the vending machines?"

"Opposite way of the elevators. Want to come?"

"Sure." I climb off the bed trying to make sure that I don't knock the plates off the bed. He grabs my hand helping me off the bed before we head towards the door. On the way out, I reach for my wallet that is sticking out of my purse. Alex tugs my hand away when he notices what I am reaching for.

I turn to look at him and he gives me a dirty look.

"You don't need that, I got this." Alex says. I go to grab it with my other hand, but he grabs my other wrist pulling it away as well.

"Alex!" I say, not liking that I can't grab my wallet. I am getting pulled closer and closer to him as he is walking backwards to the door.

"Listen to me woman, I got this." Alex reaches behind him to pull the door open. He pushes me out into the hall before the door closes behind him. Now I really can't grab anything to help pay for our drinks.

"Aren't you wrestlers supposed to be eating healthy?" I ask randomly.

"We do during training. We all promised that this weekend would be splurge days, so we are enjoying the heck out of it."

"What kind of diet do you stick to?"

"Why do you want to know what I eat?"

"I need to be on a diet." I say, patting my stomach.

"If you need to be on a diet, I can fly to the moon." Alex says as he pushes me down a hall and into the first room on the right that is filled with different vending machines.

"You can do anything you put your mind to."

"Psh, like they will let me go to the moon. But come on, how awesome would that be?"

"You would find it amazing." I say looking over the different snack choices before moving over to the two soda machines they have.

"Like you won't?"

"Oh, I would find it absolutely amazing." I look over the vending machine as Alex inserts his money.

"Would you be able to handle it?" Alex asks as he pushes the Mountain Dew button.

"That's why they have the training. You like Mountain Dew?" I ask, intrigued because that is the soda of my choice.

"It's my anti-drug." Alex says.

"You know it's rumored to decrease a man's sperm count."

"Well, I lost my thirst for it. Here." Alex hands the bottled drink to me.

"Yes!" I say before he puts more money into the machine pushing the Pepsi button this time.

"Did you say that so I wouldn't want to drink it?"

"It wasn't intended for that sole purpose, but it just happened to go that way."

"I'm curious if that is even true…"

"Look it up on Google, they know everything." I say as he grabs his Pepsi in the basket below. As we walk back to my room, Alex is glued to his phone doing research.

"It doesn't say if it does or doesn't, I don't want to risk it on my spermies." Alex says as I burst into laughter. I would have done a spit take if I had a drink in my mouth.

"I have never heard a man say that word. Please use little soldiers from now on." I say as I get comfortable on my bed. I rest my soda between my legs so I can hold it.

"I'll try. What are we watching?" Alex asks as he places his soda on the nightstand beside him and puts his plate in his lap.

"Criminal Minds, I'm addicted to this show."

"Gideon or Del Rossi?"

"Either, you?"

"They both fit well, it's hard to pick which one is better because all episodes of this show are so good." Alex says.

"I've seen this episode, but it never gets old."

"Don't ruin it, I haven't seen it yet." Alex says.

"I may have to ruin it." I say as I pull the top bun off my cheeseburger to take the lettuce and tomato off.

"What are you doing?"

"I don't like lettuce or tomato on my cheeseburger."

"It's good for you though."

"I know, but I just don't like it on my cheeseburger."

"Fine, more for me then." He grabs it off my plate and puts it on his cheeseburger.

"Have it all if you want." I say as I put the bun back onto my burger before I begin eating it.

We eat our lunch while watching the episode of Criminal Minds, but the time did not allow us to finish the episode. It had gotten to the time that we had to go to Family Feud. By that time, I was folded into Alex's embrace with his arm slumped over my shoulder with a firm grip on my bicep to hold me close. My head rested against where his arm and shoulder connected.

"God, I gotta get going." Alex says in a dreadful voice after he checks the time on his phone.

"Yeah, I don't want you to be late."

"You're making me late."

"Don't blame me." I sit up from his embrace even though I want to sit like this for the rest of the night.

"I will and I can." Alex says as he stands up. He moves both of our empty plates to the desk that hasn't been used all weekend. I slide to the edge of the bed to slide my shoes back on. I follow him out of the room and we speed walk down to where this Family Feud is to take place. Alex makes a beeline onto the stage where the other wrestlers are already at. I stand in the back of the room watching fans one by one get chosen for the fan team to play.

Needless to say, the team Alex is on has me laughing due to their stupidity. It was Alex, Rob, Jim, another wrestler by the name Eric and one girl named Jennifer. The game lasted longer than any of them expected.

I hang back waiting for Alex to meet me. While Alex is trying to make it to me, he keeps getting stopped by fans for pictures or to have a discussion. I smile, he has fans. Will I be ok with this happening to him frequently? By the time he makes it to me, the fans are pretty much all cleared out. Now, they have to turn this banquet hall into game night.

"They are setting up for game night, you want to go get Chris while I stay here to help them set up?"

"Yeah, I guess he must be dying of boredom from having to be locked up all day."

"It'll be good for him to come hang with us."

"Good for you or him?" I joke.

"Me." Alex says, smirking.

"I'll be back." I say as I walk out of the room to let Alex help them set up game night, I try to remember how to get to the banquet room I had just left. I head to Chris' room, knocking on the door not expecting him to answer the door anytime soon.

"Hold on!" Chris exclaims from inside. I patiently wait for him looking around seeing numerous people walking around and smile as they all walk by. I notice when the door opens and begins shutting. I grab a hold of the door before it shuts all the way and try to help Chris who is using his wheelchair, surprisingly. "Where's Alex?"

"He said he was going to help set the games up."

"Alex never helps set anything up."

"He may have changed. Are you even going to be able to perform these games?" I ask grabbing the two handles of the wheelchair to begin pushing him.

"I will sure as heck try my best."

"I wonder what games there will be."

"I hope they are fun ones, and ones that I can at least play." Chris says.

"Just try to have fun, it's the last night on the cruise." I say smiling and hope he won't be a Debbie Downer all night. I know that Chris usually isn't like that.

"I'm the life of the party, I have fun everywhere."

"I bet you are." I push him down a ramp before making a sharp turn to go down the hall, almost tipping him.

"Are you trying to kill me?" Chris asks, his knuckles turning white from clenching tightly on the arm rests.

"No. I promise I have pushed people in wheelchairs before, you have been in them before." I say.

"Without any accidents?"

"Besides that one time where," I begin to say jokingly.

"Don't try to bust my balls."

"Okay okay, I've never wrecked a wheelchair and haven't had any complaints thus far from anyone including you."

"I guess I'm more nervous with us being on a boat and rolling away, specifically overboard."

"I won't allow it to happen. If it does, I will jump in after you again." I say as I open the door. I pull him into the room where the game night will be taking place.

Chapter Eighteen:

When I walk in with Chris, I see Alex jump to his feet the moment he sees us. Alex was sitting at a table with Jim, Rob, and another girl I haven't met yet.

"Why is he sitting with them?" Chris asks me. Alex moves a chair away from the table to accommodate the wheelchair Chris is in.

"I don't know Chris, maybe it was assigned that way." I say not understanding what his problem is with sitting with Jim and Rob.

"Hey bud." Alex steps aside to let me push Chris into the spot he just cleared.

"Hey Alex, Jim, Rob, Jane." Chris says, nodding to those that are sitting around the table.

"Hi Jane, I'm Tara." I say locking the wheelchair in place before leaning over the circular table to shake her hand.

"Nice to meet you." She says smiling as we shake hands.

"I got you something." Alex says excitedly. He removes his hand from behind his back. Alex is holding a duplicate plush dinosaur of the one I had bought Xavier. "Now, you and Xavier will have matching dinosaurs." Alex whispers. I smile at the reasoning behind the gift opposed to the gift itself.

"You like dinosaurs?" Chris asks, looking up at me with a questionable look.

"No, but Xavier does. Alex bought me a dinosaur to match Xavier's." I explain as I hold it between my two hands. Alex smiles widely in excitement that I like it, "Thank you Alex, it is very sweet." I say smiling as I play with the dinosaur's fake horn.

Alex smiles and seems very proud of himself. Alex pulls out a chair for me to sit and pushes it in as I sit down. I put my purse between my feet as Alex sits down beside me.

"Who's Xavier?" Jim asks, confused.

"My son." I say truthfully.

"Then why did you tell me it was complicated?" He asks.

"He was adopted. He was her sister's son, but she died during childbirth." Alex answered for me. The table went silent.

"Well, now that I have killed the mood. Should I just leave or-" I trail off starting to collect my things to leave thinking that my sappy sad story killed everyone's mood to play.

"Hold on right there, pretty thing. That didn't kill the mood. That's sad, yes. But kudos to you for stepping up. Now Alex," Jim says as he turn his attention from me to squarely look at Alex. Jim points the mouth part of his beer bottle towards Alex, "You got to step up your game. Responsibilities, you've heard of those right?" Jim asks. I didn't think Jim was that much older than us, but he was giving off this big brother vibe.

"Yes, I agreed to adopt him if we were to get that far."

"Seriously?" Chris asks, shocked.

"That's great, Alex. You have to realize how lucky you are.

184

She doesn't need you. She has lasted-" Jim says, then turns to me, "How old is the boy?"

"Six."

"Six years as a single mom. You need to prove to her that you are worth holding on to and that you aren't going anywhere. She has been able to do it all by herself for this long, she knows that she doesn't need a man to survive. Those late night feedings are a real pain. She doesn't need you to add any problems to her life, being a parent is hard enough." Jim rambles.

"Guys, I'm right here." I say as I feel like I am imposing on the brotherly advice.

"I know, she's a hard worker and can make it work with or without me. I'm thankful she's even giving me a chance." Alex says with a genuine smile, his hand grabbing mine and giving it a firm squeeze. He brings my hand to rest in his lap, I look at him and he is nothing but smiles.

"Not to change the subject, but how does this game night go?" I ask not wanting to discuss this anymore. I look at the number six in the middle of the table.

"There are going to be numerous games where we are competing against the other tables for points." Rob explains.

"What games are we going to play, or do we not know? I hope that beer drinking is one since it seems you can handle your beer." I joke, getting Jim to laugh.

"What am I good at?" Alex asks.

"Annoyance." Chris answers.

"Coming from the cripple." Alex states.

"Guys, take this out in the games." Jim says.

"They are about to announce them." Rob said, nodding towards the stage. I see the blonde man that I know as Alex's boss, I think his name is Mr. Henry, and a female climb up a couple steps onto the stage.

"I hope it isn't trivia." I say.

"Why?" Alex asks.

"I suck at trivia."

"I'm sure you're good at some things in trivia like music." Jim says.

"It definitely won't be wrestling." Chris says. I smack him playfully.

"Shut up!"

"What? It's true." Chris shrugs, he did have a point though.

"May I get everyone's attention." Mr. Henry said over the sound system, getting our whole table to look at him.

"That's your boss, right?" I lean forward to ask Alex.

"Yep, and the chick is my boss too. Her name is Donna." Alex whispers back and I simply nod my head before sitting back up straight.

"Okay, it's going to be simple. You all are now separated into groups by table so always remember that and me or Donna will keep a tally of points that are given to each table on this board. The prize is half of the entry money."

"We're going to win this!" Chris says as he sits forward smacking the table.

"We will, calm down." I say turning from looking at Chris to Alex, "Entry money?"

"Don't worry about it, I got you covered." Alex says smirking, I give him a dirty look. He added, "You should thank me and not be giving me that evil eye of yours."

"Thanks, Alex." I say smiling.

"There will be six games since there are six tables, each person must compete as best as they can. As for scoring, the table that wins gets six points and the last place gets one. Now for the games, we will be playing limbo, musical spoons, passing the fruit, have you ever, Simon says and twister."

"How do you play some of those games?" I ask, I never heard of a couple of them.

"We will instruct you on how to play the game before the game starts." Mr. Henry says.

"This is going to be fun." Alex said excitedly.

"First up, limbo. We will line you up by table number, and one by one go under the pole until there are two left from each table then we will go by twos. You must completely go under the pole without touching it or the ground. Let's do this." Donna says as everyone stands up at their tables. Alex and I slide out of the way and push our chairs in to allow Chris to roll through. Since we are table six, we are the last table to go under the pole. We put Chris first, then it is Alex, me, Jim, Jane then Rob.

"This is going to be easy." Chris says as he rolls himself under the pole being nowhere close to where it is positioned. We all go through, and no one is knocked out that round. It isn't until the pole is lowered two more times, but it isn't all one table that is getting knocked out but at least people are getting eliminated from the game.

"Dude, help." Chris says as he faces the pole that is level with his eyes. I swear his eyes go cross eyed staring at the pole.

"How?" Alex asks.

"Never mind, next time." Chris says as he rolls himself forward and ducks down under the pole not to get eliminated. Alex, I, Jim, and Jane proceed through under the pole only for Rob to get knocked out unfortunately.

The pole is lowered again, more people are knocked out

Suplexed Into Love

getting two at every table now except ours. Chris stares at the pole that is now lower than prior, "Alex, lean me back so I can get through this."

"Bud, I don't think you can get through lean back or not." Alex says as Chris growls from frustration.

"Dang chair." Chris says as he turns and rolls himself back to the table allowing Alex and I to go through without a problem, but Jim and Jane can't make it through.

"Now we are down to two people per table. If you have three, pick the best two in your group to go under. Now the two of you MUST go under together." Mr. Henry instructs. I look at Alex more nervous having to go under with him. I am more afraid that I will mess it up. We watch as the tables in front of us go under the pole, only two tables get eliminated unfortunately. It is our turn.

"Let's do this high school style." He says, sticking his hand out. I grab it as we step closer to the pole.

"Don't mess this up." I joke as we both do our thing with our hands attached. We clear the pole and stand back up on the other side. We both look back at the pole we had just cleared. Alex rests his hand on my waist as we watch the pole lower again, "I don't think I can do that."

"You can, come on." Alex says, pulling me around the pole to watch the other tables trying to go under the pole. All but one other table got eliminated leaving it to us to either make it and go another round or get eliminated and become second place. I was suddenly more nervous knowing it is up to Alex and me to do this. I look at Alex to say 'I can't do this' but he put his finger to my lips.

"Whatever happens, we will be second automatically." Alex says, giving me a confident smile. He grabs my hand as we step up to the pole slowly trying to maneuver our bodies under it. Alex then loses his balance and falls all the way back to where he is laying on his back, but his legs are propped up bent at the knee.

"Dang, flexible much?" I am shocked that he is able to bend like that. I look down at him from the other side of the pole with our hands still connected.

"Well, you know." He shrugs with a laughing smile. I help him up to his feet as Donna writes five points under our table number, "I love how you were afraid you were going to mess up and I did." Alex says, wrapping his arm around me to lead me back to our table.

"It is quite comical." I say with a laugh.

"Table one is officially our enemy." Alex says as he pulls my seat out for me and he sits down beside me.

"But it was a close game between you two." Jim says as he reaches across the table to give us fist bumps.

Chapter Nineteen:

As we sit at our table, I look around the room filled with circular tables that have fans and wrestlers occupying them. Donna is tallying up the points when Chris is handed one spoon.

"Only one?" Chris asks picking up the single utensil to stare at it.

"Let them explain the game." I say as the game was then explained by Mr. Henry. The game is much like musical chairs but whoever ends up with the spoon when the music is cut off is knocked out, it seems simple enough.

Chris starts off the first round. That round, Rob is eliminated. The music starts up again. This time it lands on Alex, but he tosses it back to me where it lands in my hands.

"You're out." Alex points at me.

"No, you are." Jim said.

"She's holding the spoon though." Alex retorts. I roll my eyes, I push myself back away from the table and hand the spoon to Alex for the next round.

The very next round, he did it again to Jane. The only people left are Chris, Alex, and Jim. I sit there watching the three men at our table playing. I look around at the other tables to see who our competition might be.

Chris ends up being the last man standing, he rolls himself to the table that is placed in the middle of the room. He has to compete against the five other competitors.

Chris plays against them, but all we can do is watch intently in hopes that Chris will be the last man standing. With each round, a sigh of relief comes over us when he doesn't lose. When it is his turn to be out, I grab Alex's shoulder. Alex turns around to look at me with a smile. We both knew that we just got second place again. We got another five points. Chris rolls himself back to our table and we each give him a hi-five.

"Next game is 'pass the fruit,' and I can assure that you all have played this at some point in your life." Donna says over the sound system as Jim is handed an orange.

"An orange? I've played with a cucumber though." Jane said.

"Cucumber? What party was that at?" Jim asked.

"An adult party...shut up!" Jane says as her cheeks begin turning red.

"Have you ever played?" Alex asks, looking at me.

"Once. Haven't played since then so I don't know how good I'll be." I say.

"You're with us sweetie, we got this." Rob says as we are instructed to line up and the person at the front of the line must have the fruit.

"Chris, why don't you have the fruit first since you're the cripple." Rob says as he grabs the fruit from Jim and takes it to Chris.

"Of course, why not? When in doubt, go with the cripple."

191

Chris says, grabbing the fruit from Rob. Chris rests the fruit in his lap and rolls himself to the front of the line. Which put Alex second in line now.

"Switch with me." Alex says man-handling me to position me in between him and Chris.

"Why?" I asked.

"I don't want to get that close to him, he may kiss me." Alex said.

"Oh, I'll definitely kiss you and I'll make sure there's tongue." Chris jokingly purses his lips.

"But you're OK getting that close to Jim?" I say as we both look at Jim. Jim gives us both a smile.

"I don't mind. I thought you'd be more comfortable with Chris." Jim states as Alex then manhandles me back to my original spot.

"No hanky panky." Alex says, pointing between Jim and me.

"I promise." I say.

"I don't. We will totally kiss." Jim said.

"Oh yes." I say as Jim pulls out some Chapstick.

"Got to make sure my lips aren't dry. Does anyone have some gum?"

"I'm eating the last piece of my gum." I state.

"It'll be in my mouth soon." Jim says with a wink. I look over to Alex who does not look amused, and I can tell he was getting aggravated with our joking manner. "I just hope you slip me a little tongue." Jim added. I notice Alex then clench his jaw and his fists tightly shut momentarily before he loosens his fists.

Alex was getting jealous? He still has feelings for me and after finding out that I have Xavier. The knowledge of me being a mom didn't impact him at all. I thought, a smile coming to my face

192

that he is having jealous tendencies.

"There will always be tongue." I joke as we both let out a few more chuckles when Alex is still mad.

"Are you getting mad there, Alex?" Jim asked.

"No." Alex blurts out, his face turning red from being called out and I knew that he was lying.

"Then why are you getting so hot headed?"

"Am not." Alex said defensively.

"Everyone ready?" Mr. Henry asked over the sound system. Chris puts the orange under his chin holding it between his chin and his throat when Mr. Henry says go.

Alex leans forward to position himself to get the orange from Chris's grip. Alex successfully accomplished grasping the orange from Chris. Alex turns around to face me when we both scoot closer. I press my body against Alex's hard body. I position my neck against the orange he is holding, and I am successfully able to pick it from his throat.

I step back and the orange doesn't fall, a sigh of relief comes over me. I turn around to face Jim, we meet in the middle where he squats down to be my height. He grabs the fruit from me with his throat. I can't help but mentally scream in excitement that I was able to move the fruit from Alex to Jim. I turn around pulling Alex in for a hug. I let him go, my blue eyes meet his brown eyes and I smile. He smiles back at me, and he pulls me back in for a hug.

"I did it!" I say as I look around at the tables who are struggling to get past the second person. I see Rob passing the fruit to Jane now, "We might win!"

"Table six came in first, who will be second?" Mr. Henry said. We both jump in excitement watching the other tables finish up slowly. "Table one coming in second."

"Darn that table one, we have to beat them." Alex says as he pulls my seat out and pushes it in as I sit down. Alex slides into the seat next to me.

"Were you getting jealous of Jim and I?" I ask curiously.

"No." Alex says shifting his eyes before he makes eye contact with me, I know he is lying.

Chapter Twenty:

~~~

We sit at our table listening to the leader board being announced again. After the leader board is listed off, the next game is then introduced.

"Next game is 'Never Have I?' Everyone stand up, sit down if what I say fits you." Donna said.

"I guess you can't play handicap." Alex says, looking at Chris as we all stand up to play this game.

"Dang, good luck guys!" Chris said.

"Sit down if you cry during Disney movies." Mr. Henry said.

"Thank God Chris isn't playing, he would be out already." Alex said sarcastically.

"The Lion King is very emotional." Chris said.

"How so?" Alex asked.

"Mufasa died." Chris says as I can't help but to laugh.

"I cried at that part too," pausing for effect, "when I was five."

"Difference, five and thirty something." Alex says and I can tell Chris is embarrassed. I know Chris well enough, he will get pay back. The game progresses, it is down to Jim, Alex, and

I at our table. I look over at table one seeing only two people remaining.

"Sit down if you're wearing underwear." Mr. Henry says. I sit down, and I notice that neither Alex nor Jim sat down.

"Alex!" I gasp, shocked that he wasn't.

"What? I'm not." Alex said.

"He didn't tell you?" Chris said.

"No, but now I know." I am thankful that I didn't know, but I will now have to live with knowing this tidbit about Alex. I turn to where Jim is still standing too. "Jim, you're not wearing any either?" I ask. I would have thought he would have been classier, but Rob now seems classier than I thought.

"You think I could wear these tight jeans with underwear?" Jim asks.

"Well, he's got a point." Jane says as everyone at the table turns to look at her. She is distracted by twirling the straw in her cup.

"You noticed?" Jim asked.

"Who doesn't?" Chris asked. We all then turn our attention to him, and he simply shrugs, "What?"

"We might have this, there is only one person left at table one." Alex said.

"We got this." Jim said fist bumping Alex.

"Sit down if you have never kissed a guy." Donna said. The last guy that was remaining at table one sits down, and Jim acts fast. Grabbing Alex by the back of the head and pulling him in. Jim plants a huge kiss on Alex's lips. Alex shoves at Jim to get off him.

"Jim!" Alex exclaims, wiping at his mouth.

"Table six is our winner, congrats guys." Mr. Henry says as Alex and Jim sit down in their seats. When Alex goes to sit down Chris kicks the chair out from beneath him. Alex falls flat on his butt; he looks up at Chris and I am biting my lip trying not to laugh.

"Hakuna Matata beotch." Chris says to Alex. Alex looks up at Chris with a shocked expression, I can't help but to laugh more.

"You whore." Alex said, reaching for the table. I stick my hand out to help him, he looks at my hand then up to me, "Thanks." Alex grabs my hand and uses it to help himself to his feet. He pulls his seat back in to sit down without falling yet again.

"Next up is Simon Says, come on up here." Mr. Henry said. We all moan, no one wants to do this game. We all move up to the empty dance floor in front of the stage that the two bosses stand on. "I'm sure you all know how to play this game, so I'm just going to begin. Simon says, touch your toes."

"Easy as pie." Chris said. Chris re-positions himself in his wheelchair until he can touch his toes on the foot that is locked in the splint.

"Do jumping jacks." Donna says as a few people start to do jumping jacks. Those people are being listed off because they are now eliminated from the game.

"This is ridiculous." Chris said.

"What? That they did the jumping jacks without Simon Says being said or that you're like Gumby?" Alex said. Alex looks up to Chris from his bent over position.

"You'll be Gumby here in a moment." Chris threatens before he turns his wheelchair around. Chris wheels himself back to the empty table.

"Simon says do jumping jacks." Donna says as Alex and I begin doing the jumping jacks.

"Some date this is." Alex said.

"Date? This is a date?" I ask. I stop doing jumping jacks to look at Alex confused.

"Miss, you're out." Mr. Henry said. I look up at the stage before I look back at Alex when he stops.

"Sir, she isn't out. She only stopped because of something I had said." Alex says, I have to smile at his 'hero' moment.

"I will let this one slide. But miss, you need to be warned of that man. He may be charming, but he can be very distracting." Mr. Henry says as my face begins to burn from blushing. I begin doing jumping jacks again trying not to let what Alex said affect my gaming ability. It didn't help that I did get disqualified a couple rounds later, and Jim got disqualified on the same round.

"Come on sweetie, we will win next time." He says putting his arm around me as we walk to our table. I look back at Alex who has that same look as earlier on his face. "You want a drink?"

"Nah, I'm good." I say as we head to our table. He pulls my seat out and I sit down. I look at Chris, he looks bummed.

"What's wrong?" I ask towards Chris.

"I'm useless due to my stupid leg. I'm so bored sitting here watching you guys having fun." Chris said.

"I'm sorry. Hey, I think I have cards in my purse. Do you know how to play five card draw?" I asked.

"If you're playing five card draw, count me in." Jim said.

"You're both on. Now this is game night." Chris said with a smile. I pull out the deck of dinosaur cards from my purse. My eyes land on the dinosaur plush that Alex gave me on the table, I grab it and rest the dinosaur in my lap.

"Let's make this interesting, let's make bets. How much

money do you all have?" Jim asked.

"Um, I have forty bucks." I say as I begin pulling my wallet out.

"I can do forty." Chris says as he is shifting in his seat to pull out his wallet. Jim stands up to pull out his wallet and both men count out their cash as I shuffle the cards. We each ante up a dollar before we begin the first round of the game.

We play until we are joined by Jane and Alex, they pay their way into the game with us. The list of winners are announced, our table came in second yet again.

"Who won the most money? I'm out about thirty-eight bucks." Jim says, he looks at the two dollar bills in front of him.

"I got seventy-eight bucks." I say counting out my stack of cash.

"I invested in something good then." Jim says with a wink.

"Looks like I missed all the fun." Rob says coming back to our table.

"That you did." Chris said.

"What place did you come in?" I ask, pretending I missed the announcement.

"Second." Rob answered.

"We need to win this round to tie for first." Alex said.

"Table one is going down." Jim says as we see white tarps being placed on the floor.

"What game is this?" I ask not being able to make out what is on the tarps.

"Twister, I'm sure you all know the rules." Donna says as everyone makes it up to the numbered tarps. We all slip our shoes off to play the game more effectively. "First up is left foot on blue." Donna said, handing the spinner to Mr. Henry to spin.

"I can do that!" Chris says excitedly. He scoots to the edge of his wheelchair, and he stretches his left foot as far as he can so it will land on the blue circle.

"I'm impressed Chris, so truly impressed." Alex sarcastically said.

"I'm impressed honestly." Chris says as Mr. Henry grabs the microphone from Donna.

"Right foot on red." Mr. Henry said. I move my right foot to the red circle. I look up from the red circle, my eyes stare deep into Alex's eyes since we are now facing each other. I look over to see Chris with his tongue stuck out trying to figure out a way to play.

"Chris, it'll be safer for you not to play." I said.

"Dang it, I hate this leg." Chris begins to mumble as he rolls himself back to the table.

"Right hand on yellow." Donna reads off. I look down at the yellow circles that are between my feet. Alex leans back putting his hand on yellow while I lean forward putting my hand on yellow.

I wasn't focusing on what the other three people from our table were doing. I look up to the stage waiting for the next move to be called. I notice that my head is positioned next to Alex's crotch, instant blush.

"Boy is this awkward." I say, trying not to turn any redder from embarrassment.

"I don't mind." Alex said, giving me a wink.

"Of course you wouldn't mind." I said. I roll my eyes as we are told to put our left hand on green, which doesn't help the situation.

We have to balance off each other for the next couple of

spins to the point where Alex is laying over me to keep his hand on a spot. I look over at him, he is quite adorable as he smiles and gives me a wink.

"Sup?" He asked, giving me a nod.

"You're such a geek." I say with a laugh. I couldn't help but to think he was cute at that moment. Jim and Rob got out in the next two spins.

"More space for us!" Alex says as we are able to spread out some. Sooner rather than later both Alex and I get out, leaving Jane to stay up there to compete in the finals.

"She can't limbo, but yet can twister." Chris said, shocked.

"With limbo you can't use your arms for balance." Rob explains. Jane stands in front of the room with one other person to determine the final winner.

"It isn't balance in twister per say, it's more about flexibility. You can be as balanced as the next but if you can't twist in different positions then screw it." Jim said.

"You sound like you know these positions way too well." Alex said.

"I've been in a lot of positions if you know what I mean." Jim said with a wink.

"Oh god." I said with a roll of my eye. I am staring at the dinosaur plush that is on the table in front of me, pulling it back to rest in my lap.

"You want to try one sweetie?" Jim asks. He sips his beer as Rob nudges him to shut up. I glance up at Alex who has his fist clenched and his jaw locked.

"No thanks, the ones I know aren't that bad." I said.

"Do we have to talk about what sex positions we know?" Chris asked.

"I wasn't talking about sex, jeez you pervert." I say jokingly.

"I think you're the only one not thinking about sex at this table." Rob said.

"I'm not." Alex says and he looks more relaxed now.

"I thought as a wrestler you all need flexibility to perform some of those moves." I said playing with the plush toy in my lap.

"We do to an extent. There are some men that are nothing but muscles and can't be as flexible as us small guys." Chris explained.

"Its well-known muscles can't stretch." I said jokingly.

"What do you do?" Rob asked.

"I work as a manager in training of health services and EMT response at the Resort. I am also a registered nurse." I answered.

"She's also my beotch." Chris said smiling.

"Am not, I'm the only one that took pity on you." I stated.

"No one likes you, Chris." Alex joked.

"Same with you Alex." Chris said.

"We have a tie between table one and table six, this one is for a tie breaker." Donna announced.

"Dude, it's a tie!" Alex said excitedly.

"The tie breaker game will be a rock paper scissors tournament." Mr. Henry says as we all get up to join Jane. I look over at the other six people up there. I recognize two of the members of the other table as Jennifer and Eric from the Family Feud game.

"We are going one by one to play a round. If you lose, you're out. If you win, stay put and go against the next competitor." Donna explains, somehow Alex and I end up being the last two in our line.

"This is ridiculous. Who has a talent in rock, paper, or

scissors?" Alex asked.

"I do. I have yet to lose a game." I state.

"Seriously?" Alex asked, impressed and intrigued.

"You'll see." I say as it gets down to Alex and me. I step up to be toe to toe with a man that is obviously way taller than me. I look up at the taller man, his face is stone. He is ready to play and knock me out.

"Ready?" Mr. Henry asks. We both nod when Mr. Henry said "Rock-Paper-Scissors" as we hit our hands three times then the last one is our decision. I decide on paper to defeat the rock that the man had put.

"That is just luck." Alex said.

"Just wait." I say as I turn around seeing Jennifer step up to compete with me. We go through the motions to do the game, and win.

"Two for two, still think it's luck though." Alex said.

"You'll see." I say turning around ready for the next round beating the last member of the other table.

"Dang, try it on me." Alex says as I turn around and win yet again.

"Told you." I say with a smile.

"That you did." He says smiling. Alex grabs my hand, pulls me closer to him. His arm wrapped around my waist as I stand beside him.

"The winner is table six. They each win a portion of half of the entry money."

"Why are we getting only half of the entry money?" Chris asks as he rolls his wheelchair to the front of the room to be with us.

"The other half is being donated to the Ronald McDonald house." Donna answers.

"I can't honestly take my portion of the money. I will feel guilty, and they need the money more than I do." I say. I already feel bad that Alex paid however much to get me into the game night.

"I feel the same." Alex agrees. I look back at him with a smile, it feels good that he backed me up and that my character judgment hasn't done me wrong.

"Speak for yourself, I have medical bills." Chris said.

"Christopher!" I gasp.

"What?" Chris shrugs his shoulders, then he finally gives in, "Fine, I'll donate my portion too." Chris says as he rolls away. Jim, Rob, and Jane agree to donate their portion to the Ronald McDonald house as well. I had the most fun playing the games tonight with everyone. Alex and I walk back to our table where I pick up my purse and grab the plush dinosaur that Alex bought me.

Chapter Twenty-One:

Alex and I are gathering our things from the table to take Chris back to his room before we are to go back up to our rooms.

"Can you guys hurry up?" Chris asks impatiently.

"What is your rush? You're just going back to your room." Alex says.

"Batman is about to come on." Chris says excitedly as he is rolling himself towards the door.

"Oh, how could I forget?" Alex says, rolling his eyes. Alex grabs my hand, our fingers interlacing as our arms rest between our bodies. We walk behind Chris out of the room and towards his guest room.

"I had fun tonight." I said smiling.

"Me too. I always have fun when I'm with you." Alex said.

"Oh god, I do NOT want to hear this." Chris said, trying to roll himself faster.

"Hear what?" I ask curiously as Alex and I walk up the two steps next to the ramp.

"Your mushiness, it's sickening." Chris said.

"Mushiness? Is that even a word?" Alex asks.

"It should be. The act of being mushy." Chris said.

"When will that ever be used?" I ask.

"I just did." Chris said.

"But you're weird." I said.

"I'm weird? Look at who you're holding hands with." Chris says as I look over to Alex, I can't help but to smile. Alex just makes me happy.

"We are all weird in our own ways." I say as we turn down the hall getting to Chris's door.

"What makes you weird?" Alex asks.

"I'm with you, isn't that weird enough?" I ask as Chris bursts into laughter. Chris has to calm down from laughter before he can even try to unlock the door.

"I should have seen that coming." Alex says with a chuckle and shakes his head in disbelief that he fell for that. I open the door, and hold it open, so Chris can roll in. Alex walks in behind Chris, I step in the room and the door closes behind me. I stand at the end of the bed watching Chris move himself over to his bed, and once he is situated, he flips his television on.

"Do you need anything?" I ask, reaching for a pillow and propping it under his leg.

"Nope." Chris says as he sets the remote down when he gets to the right channel.

"Tara, he has Batman. He's good." Alex says as he grabs my hand and begins to tug me towards the door.

"Do you need help packing tomorrow?" I ask turning back around to continue the conversation. Alex walks back to let the hands that are connected fall back to our side.

"If I do, I won't ask you." Chris said.

"I'll help you, don't worry." Alex says as he grabs my other hand and pulls me to the door.

"Night Chris, hope you had fun!" I say looking back at him momentarily. Alex pulls me out of the room into the hallway.

We stand outside of Chris's room; Alex stands in front of me as I am trying to look anywhere but into his eyes. I feel nervous and awkward at the moment.

"Are you tired?" Alex asks, feeling his fingers brush through my hair.

"No, you?" I ask. I fix the strand of hair that is now messed up. We are both smiling, and it still seems very awkward.

"No, you want to go for a walk?" Alex asked.

"I would love that." I answer. Alex grabs my hand interlacing his fingers with mine. "Thanks for the dinosaur, it's really cute that you did that."

"Now the trick question, what's cuter? Me or that dinosaur?" Alex asks as we step down a couple of steps that leads us out to the main deck.

"Definitely the dinosaur." I joke.

"I could say the same." Alex says, I look at Alex giving him a shocked expression before I start laughing.

"You really impressed me at those games tonight."

"Well, I tried." Alex says as he blushes a tad. We reach the deck not seeing anyone around besides the ring and the tent.

"Does your company do a lot of charity work?" I ask as I let him lead me to the black metal rail that wraps around the ring. It was set up as a barricade for the fans to line up to watch the matches and for the fans' safety.

"We try our best to give back as much as we can. I love it." Alex says. He lets go of my hand, I watch as he puts his foot on the railing and swings his foot over the top. He looks like he is riding the rail before he swings his other leg over.

"What are you doing?" I ask in a whisper. I look around to make sure no one is truly around.

"Going to get in the ring, come on." He says in a whisper back and a big grin on his face.

"Aren't we going to get in trouble?" I ask, looking around again. I feel him grasp my chin and turn my face to stare deep into his big brown eyes.

"Look who you're with. Do you think you'll get in trouble when I'm around?" He asks, when I went to answer he stops me, "Don't answer that. I'm the talent, so we won't get in trouble for being in the ring." Alex said as I let out a sigh. I still worry but trust Alex enough after tonight. He helps me over the railing and we both climb into the ring.

"Why didn't we go through the curtain?" I ask, trying to get used to being in the ring. I begin to spin around to see what it is like to be in the center of the ring. I turn around to look at Alex, who is sitting on the top turnbuckle.

"That's too easy. What do you think of being in the ring?" Alex asks.

"It's definitely different. Not as soft as I thought." I said.

"Lay down."

"Excuse me?" I'm not sure if I heard him right.

"Lay down, to look at the stars." Alex says. He points up at the night sky as he jumps off the top turnbuckle.

"Oh." I nod. I slowly lay down on the mat and he lays beside me. I am pulled into his embrace where I rest my head on his shoulder and his arm wraps tightly around me.

"That's the North Star." Alex says pointing up to the sky full of stars. I wasn't quite sure which star he was pointing to.

"How can you tell if it's the North Star?" I ask, looking up at him.

"It's always the brightest star and it's always North from where you are. The North Star can lead you home, so we are going that way."

"So, there is no hardcore evidence that it is the North Star, so that can be it or that one." I say pointing to other stars in the sky to make my point.

"You've made your point. See that's the big dipper." Alex says as he begins pointing out other things in the sky I can never find normally.

"How do you know all this?" I ask as I cuddle closer to him to get more body warmth.

"Took Astrology 105 in college." Alex says, smirking.

"What did you major in again?" I ask.

"Liberal Arts. You want to learn a few moves?" Alex asks, running his hand through my hair. I look up at Alex, unsure if I heard him right as I roll over to look up at him more comfortably. My chin rests on my hands that lay on his chest.

"Why would I want to?" I ask sarcastically.

"To beat me up when you want and to protect yourself."

"From who?" I ask.

"Bad guys like me." Alex says, he runs his hand through the roots of my hair.

"You're not bad. You may be annoying but not bad."

"You crack me, so I'm not that bad."

"That you're not. You're too good." I say smiling. "I meant bad guys like thugs."

"Will I get hurt?" I ask.

"No, I'm the professional and I'll take all the hits." Alex says as he moves so he can jump up to his feet by thrusting and pushing himself up.

"Impressive." I say as I sit up, he turns around with a smile on his face.

"Give it a try." Alex said, leaning against the ropes.

"I can't do that, I'm not that talented."

"It takes time and practice, here." Alex says, sticking his hand out to help me to my feet.

"You won't get hurt, will you?" I ask worriedly.

"Psh, don't worry." He says as he turns me around. His arms wrap around me, "If he attacks you from behind, what would you do?" Alex asks as I think about it for a moment. I elbow him in the face, step on his toe, then nudge him in the gut. I turn around now that I broke his grip. I go to knee him where it counts; he grabs my leg, "Whoa! Not there. I'm not wearing the proper protection for that. Let me teach you a move that would do just as well. It's good to turn around to see what they look like but if they have their hands in an area that you are able to grab them and flip them, do that. Try it." Alex says, sticking his arm over my shoulder. I look at his arm, then at him.

"I'm not that strong." I say.

"It's not about strength, it's adrenaline. Do you want me to make you angry? I can piss anyone off, including you." Alex says.

"I bet you could, but how would I be able to flip you over?" I ask.

"Go with what is natural." Alex said. I begin to feel butterflies in my stomach as I grab a hold of his wrist and try to turn it in a way to get him to flip over my body. He does the flip by himself, he lands flat on his butt then he lays back to a laying position.

"Oh my god, are you okay?" I ask, dropping to my knees

beside him.

"Got you!" He said, chuckling. I playfully smack him for scaring me like that. I turn around wanting to get out of the ring, I feel his arm snake around my waist and pull me down to the mat. Oddly, it doesn't hurt when I land flat on the ring below. Alex rolls on top of me, straddling my waist and begins tickling me.

A beam of light shines on us, we stop to look where it came from. A security guard stands on the other side of the railing staring at us. "What are you two doing in there? You two got to go."

"Way to go, Alex." I say looking back at Alex. He looks down at me with a smile.

"You know me too well." Alex says, smiling more as he gets to his feet. Alex helps me to my feet. He helps me over to the ropes where he steps on the bottom rope and holds the middle rope up so I can slide between the two. I sit down on the apron and climb down from there. Alex climbs out of the ring and jumps off the apron. We walk through the curtain being greeted by the security guard. The guard escorts us back up to our rooms. When we get inside, Alex walks through the connecting door. We couldn't help but burst into laughter.

"Always getting us in trouble, I swear." I say smiling. I walk over to my bed and sit down. Alex leans against the door staring at me.

"What can I say? I'm just bad to the bone." Alex said with a shrug and a smile.

"I doubt that. I think that you have a good side." I said.

"Only around you."

"I doubt that since you just got me in trouble." I said, smirking.

"I got you in trouble because I like you." Alex says as I look up to him. Alex is looking down at his feet.

"Pull the pig tails of the one you like, huh?" I ask as he looks up at me making eye contact.

"What they say is true then." Alex said with a bright smile.

"You want to join me; I think Batman is still on." I said.

"Which one is it?" Alex asks as he walks further into the room to look at the television. I turn it on and flip through the channels until I get to the movie channel.

"It looks like Batman Begins with the Scarecrow." I said.

"You watch Batman?"

"Duh, I told you Xavier is obsessed with Batman. I have seen them all more than a gazillion times."

"Which one is your favorite?" Alex asked, looking over at me.

"Dark Knight is my favorite thus far." I said.

"Move, I want to sit and watch." Alex said.

"Hold on." I said moving to give him enough room to lay beside me. He climbs onto the bed beside me, he lays down and wraps his arm around me. Alex pulls me closer to him, we are laying like we were out in the ring. "I liked the Scarecrow character though."

"I've seen scarier creatures."

"But I think he is scarier than what they had in the original movies." I say.

"I like the Batman movie with Adam West."

"That movie always makes me laugh. My favorite part is where he's running with the bomb and afterwards, he is like 'Some days you just can't get rid of a bomb.'" I laugh thinking about it, and he laughs too. Alex leans his head against mine making us closer.

Chapter Twenty-One

"Do you watch Family Guy?"

"Yes, Adam West makes that show. Not as much as Herbert the Pervert or Bruce." I say.

"Herbert the Pervert is amazing, 'Oh No!'" Alex says doing it in Bruce's voice, getting me to laugh.

"They are so mean to Meg in that show." I say, smiling as I make eye contact with him. We are mere inches apart from each other. I want to give him a kiss but feel that it is too soon or too forward of me.

"But yet you are laughing about it."

"Yes, I am. Have you seen the one with the horse?"

"With crazy eyes?"

"Yeah." I said laughing.

"I think I've seen every episode."

"Me too." I say as I move closer to him. My head rests against his chest; Alex reaches down to pull the covers over us when it gets cold in the room. My eyes close on their own, I end up falling asleep wrapped in his arms without knowing it.

Chapter Twenty-Two

❧

I wake up to the sound of a phone ringing. My eyes flutter open, I realize that it is my phone that is ringing. I see Alex lean back and smack at the nightstand. When his hand lands on my phone, he grabs the phone then hands it to me.

"It's Chris." Alex says in a mumble. Alex runs a hand along his face, probably to wake himself up more.

"Why is he calling?" I was confused why he would be calling me. I answer the phone, "Chris?"

"Have you seen or heard from Alex?" Chris asks in a panic.

"He's right here, why?" I ask, my panic rising because he was in a panic.

"He was supposed to come help me pack, we are docking at noon." Chris answers, a sense of relief in his voice. I begin to calm myself down now that it wasn't anything too serious.

"What time is it?"

"Eleven."

"Oh, ok. I'll send him your way." I look at Alex. He has propped his head up with one hand. He looks at me as his fingers play with the tips of my hair.

"Thanks." Chris says and I hang up.

"Chris needs you to go help him pack, we are docking in an hour." I say.

"That quick?"

"Yep, that quick." I say.

"Alright. Don't move!" Alex says. Alex sits up, swings his legs over the edge of the bed and starts to put his shoes on.

"Where would I go? I got to pack myself." I say smiling.

"Okay. I also have your number now."

"That you do." I say as I watch him leave my room. I climb out of the bed. I call my mom and she doesn't answer. I assume she is still asleep or at the gym. "Hey mom, the boat is docking at noon. I don't know what time I will get off the boat to catch my flight. I will call you when I get to the airport. Love you."

I sit on the bed looking at the phone kind of upset that this weekend has finally come to an end. What is going to happen to Alex and me after today?

"I knew that this wasn't going to last forever." I say sadly. I set the background of my phone to a picture of Alex and I.

I stand up and pack everything that needs to be packed. An announcement comes over the intercoms and television saying that the boat is now docked and that we are welcome to stay aboard until 1500. It also said that there will be events taking place until then or we are welcome to leave whenever we feel like it.

I zip up my suitcase when I look over and see the plush dinosaur that Alex had given me. The dinosaur slumps over the edge of my purse. I smile as I go and grab it out of my purse only to hear a knock come to the door. I walk over to the door to look through the peephole. I see Alex on the other side fixing his hair. I roll my eyes as I open the door, "Hey."

"You want to go grab some lunch? Chris is waiting for us at Subway." Alex says.

"Absolutely, let me grab my stuff." I say as I walk back inside grabbing my belongings. Alex grabs my hand and leads me down to the restaurant. Chris is already sitting at a table made for four, and he is looking at his phone. "You look bored." I lean forward against the back of a silver chair. Alex stands behind me with his hands firmly gripping at my hips.

"I am. I was about to call my doctor to see if he's in." Chris says.

"Call away, we'll go order our food. What do you want?" I ask.

"Alex knows what I want." Chris says.

"I told you I can be smart." Alex says with a wink. Alex and I get in the short line. We walk through the line to build the sandwiches we want. By the time we get back to the table Chris is putting his phone down on the table.

"Is your doc in?" I ask sitting down across from Chris so he can use the chair beside him to prop his leg up.

"Yeah, he has an open spot this evening. Will you give me a ride?" Chris asks Alex.

"No problem, bro."

"What time is your flight?" I ask.

"We drove the five to six hours here; it seemed like a quick trip because Alex is a speed demon." Chris answers for them.

"I take the speed limit as a suggestion." Alex says, smirking.

"You're one of those people, huh?" I ask.

"Yep." Alex says proudly.

"Are you working tomorrow?"

"Yeah, are you working tomorrow?" Alex asks.

"You'll find out." I say smiling. I wasn't going to tell them yes or no because I knew Alex would show up if I said yes. If I said no, he would ask why I wasn't.

"I guess I will." Chris says.

"You guys have to film tomorrow even though you were just on this cruise?" I ask.

"Yeah, we film two weeks in advance sometimes. I don't know why we didn't this time." Alex says.

"So, why do you have to be there if you're injured Chris?" I ask.

"I don't know, I honestly don't want him there." Alex says.

"You could always leave." Chris says.

"But honestly." I say.

"I have to be there. I'm obligated to be there, and I have nothing else to do besides sitting at the apartment." Chris says.

"At least you do get out of the house, and you have a friend there." I say.

"Who? Alex? He doesn't count as a friend." Chris says.

"I wasn't talking about Alex; I was going to say me."

"I think I'm a good friend." Alex says.

"You are...when you are not getting them in trouble." I say.

"Did you get in trouble last night?" Chris asked Alex. Chris crosses his arms over his chest as Alex slowly bites into his sandwich.

"He got us escorted back to our rooms because he wanted to get in the ring."

"He took you into the ring? Alex! You know no one besides talent is allowed in the ring and no one is allowed in there after dark." Chris says.

"You knew we weren't supposed to be there, but you took me there anyway?" I ask, looking at Alex.

"Testing to see if you believed me and guess what? You did."

"Note to self, don't trust Alex or always question everything he says." Chris says.

"Like I do for you?" I ask him.

"Yes."

"Did you call mom?" Alex asks.

"Mom, no one told me." Chris says.

"Yes, I called mom. She didn't pick up."

"I hate when parents do that." Chris says, rolling his eyes.

"I understand your parents, I don't pick up the phone for you half the time." Alex says.

"Like this morning?"

"Yeah, I ignored you." Alex says smiling.

"So, you waited until he called me to wake me up?" I ask.

"Yeah." Alex says, smiling bigger.

"You two were sleeping together?" Chris asks, with a perked brow and his interest is piqued.

"Not sexually though." I quickly say, so he won't get the wrong idea.

"No, it was totally sexual." Alex nods his head yes.

"I'm going to believe her." Chris says as I finish my six-inch sub. I crumble up the wrapper before I take a sip of my drink.

"Thanks for believing me, Chris."

"I never believe Alex half the time." Chris says.

"Ditto." Alex says, sipping his drink too.

"Well, we gotta get going. You want to go get your things?" Chris asks Alex.

"Yeah, we should get going. I'll walk you back to your room." Alex says, looking at me.

"First, let's get Chris to his room." I say as I stand up to take care of the trash. Alex hangs onto my free hand as we escort

Chris to his room. Chris unlocks his door, and I hold it open for him. "Are you going to be able to roll your suitcase?"

"Probably not." Chris says.

"Why don't we go get our stuff then we'll come back and help you?" I ask.

"If you want." Chris said.

"Yeah, give us fifteen minutes." Alex said.

"You work fast." Chris said jokingly, nudging at Alex.

"I'm not that easy, Chris." I say, rolling my eyes. Alex rests his hand on the arch of my back and leads me out of Chris' room. "Don't you have to pack yet?" I ask as Alex closes Chris' door.

"All my things are pretty much already packed. As a wrestler, you pretty much live out of your suitcase a lot of times." Alex says as he moves his arm to wrap around me, and hangs it over my shoulder. I wrap my arm around his waist. I didn't want to bring up anything about what would happen after we leave this ship or our future because I want to enjoy the last few moments with him.

My phone begins to ring and I pick it up. "Hey, mom." I say as Alex and I stop next to the elevators. He stands there silently while I am on the phone. We wait for an elevator to come get us.

"Just got home from the gym. I'll be at the airport to pick you up, when are you supposed to land?" My mom asks.

"That'll be great mom, I'm not sure when my flight is supposed to land. I have to look at my flight information." I say.

"Okay, well text me the information. I love you, see you when you get here." My mom said.

"Love you too." I say hanging up the phone.

"When is your flight?" Alex asks as we climb onto the elevator. He leans against the railing and pulls me to stand in front of him. I lean against his hard frame.

"Three." I said.

"What are you going to do until then?" Alex asked.

"I'm probably going to check out of my room then I'll walk you and Chris to your car. Between then and when I have to leave shouldn't be that big of a time difference." I shrug.

"What are you going to do for that long though?"

"I have my iPod and I'll go through the pictures on my phone." I say.

"Actually, why don't I call Chris and tell him we'll leave at one so we can give you a ride to the airport on our way back home?" Alex suggests as we climb off the elevator to head to our rooms.

"That's up to you." I say, trying not to smile from happiness that he may want to spend more time with me.

"I'll call him, you get your things together." He says smiling. I let myself into my room and check myself out of my room via the television. I leave my key on the desk like you would do at a hotel and I grab my things heading out of my room.

Chapter Twenty-Three:

I took the elevator back down, walk out to the main deck and see a match going on. There are very few fans that are watching the match. I walk around the fans to the railing to look out at the ocean that we were just sailing on. Thoughts about this whole weekend cloud my mind.

I am sad that it has come to an end now, but I knew that it was going to end this whole time. Why am I feeling the way I feel? Is it because Alex and I had hit it off and I may not see Alex after this? My emotions are running wild.

I hope that staring at the ocean will help calm me down. It never fails that whenever I get in a down mood, being outside always helps me think and clear my mind. I am brought out of my thoughts when I feel arms wrap around me, I jump at the feeling. I turn around seeing Alex.

"How'd you know I was here?" I ask.

"You were here the other day. I figured since you weren't in your room, you'd be here. What's wrong?" Alex asks as he runs a hand through my hair. How does he know something is wrong?

"It's nothing." I say putting on a fake smile. My eyes jolt up and down, afraid to make eye contact with him. I try to put up a front that I am OK but am not.

"You know you don't have to put on a fake front for me, right?"

"I know." I say, nodding as I look down at my hands that are playing together nervously. Alex grips my chin, lifting my face up to make eye contact with him.

"You can tell me." Alex says sincerely.

"What about us?"

"What about us?" Alex asks as the one corner of his mouth perks up in a half smile.

"I had so much fun this weekend, what will happen between us after we leave this boat? Are we going our separate ways? I'm afraid of what is going to happen to us." I say embarrassed. His phone blaring from his leather jacket right when he opens his mouth to respond. Alex pulls out his phone, looks at his screen and swipes to answer it. He presses the phone to his ear, his eyes still locked with mine.

"Hey Chris...yeah...we'll be right there....no problem..." Alex says as he hangs up. Alex slides the phone back into his pocket when he looks up at me from his pocket, "Don't worry about it sweetie, I won't let you go that easy." Alex says, winking at me, "But first, we have to go get Chris. He thinks we will be late if we leave any later. Chris is insisting on leaving now." Alex says as he grabs my hand. He pulls me into his embrace for a big hug.

He holds me in his embrace for a few moments as my head rests on his chest and it feels oh so good. He then lets me go to grab my bag with his hand and my hand with the other.

"I can take care of my bag." I say.

"It's no problem." Alex says. He leads me to Chris's room, we knock on the door and it opens quicker than it ever has.

"Are you ready to go?" I ask, holding the door open as he hobbles out.

"I'll get your bag." Alex says as he walks in and grabs Chris's suitcase. I grab the handle to my suitcase that Alex had left behind.

"Are you leaving too?" Chris asks.

"Yeah, I'll walk with you guys to your car." I say.

"She's going to miss me." Alex says smiling.

"Am not." I lie, with a smile coming to my face.

"You won't miss much." Chris says. I hold the door open for Alex, he walks out rolling Chris's bag out behind him.

"I know I won't miss you since I'll probably see you tomorrow." I say as Alex steps beside me. I feel his free hand grasp mine. Our hands fall between our bodies as we begin to walk towards where we are to exit the ship.

"You'll see me too." Alex says, smirking.

"How?" I ask with a perked brow.

"I'm going to go with him."

"Great." I say. I watch Chris hobble on his crutches along the narrow ramp towards land. I want to make sure he isn't making his leg worse.

"Isn't it?" Alex asks with a cocky smile.

"Very." I say with a smile, turning my attention back to Chris. "Be careful, Chris!" I call after him. I step up to begin my journey across to land. I am mostly focused on Chris's movement. I want him to make it safely and not cause more harm to his knee. Chris makes the distance safely, stopping beside the passenger door of a green Jaguar that is parallel parked.

I open the door to the car, and help Chris get situated in the leather seat. I open the backseat, sliding the metal crutches into the vehicle and prop them up enough where they won't get crushed by the door. Alex loads Chris's bag into the trunk before the trunk is slammed shut.

I step back onto the sidewalk beside my luggage. I see Chris roll down his window, his arm resting on the window frame. Alex steps in front of me, shoving his hands in his jean's pockets. The tension between us is awkward and full of nervous energy.

"Are you sure you're going to be okay until a cab gets here?" Alex asks. He takes a step closer, our bodies are now mere inches apart. He moves his hands to rest on my hips and I feel him slightly tug me closer to him.

"Alex, I'm an adult. I can handle it." I say. I look down at my feet then up at him making eye contact.

"I bet you can. You can handle me so you'll be fine."

"I bet."

"I'll call you tonight."

"Promises, promises." I say with a nervous laugh.

"I always keep mine too." Alex says as he presses his forehead against mine.

"You say that." I say smiling, all I can do is keep eye contact with him.

"I'm not only saying that. I like you, Tara." Alex says.

"Liar." I say with a big smile. Hearing him say that makes my heart full, I am giddy.

"Kiss her already." Chris yells from the car. We both look at him and he is watching us intently from the car.

"Shut up, Gumby!" Alex yells back.

"Just do it, you idiot!" Chris says.

"I'm sorry about my immature friend." Alex says as I can't help but to giggle. I look from Chris to Alex.

"Maybe you should listen to your immature friend." I say as I see a smile spread across his lips.

"Are you okay with it?" Alex asks. I grab the back of his head and pull him in for a kiss.

"WOOO! Get it boy!" Chris exclaims, clapping. We break the kiss and Alex rolls his eyes.

"He's such a jerk." Alex says as he leans his forehead against mine.

"But he's a good friend." I say as he presses his lips against mine for another small kiss.

"Come on, Alex! Quit making out with the girl!" Chris yells.

"I have to go; my Gumby is calling." Alex says.

"Go. We'll talk when you 'call' me." I say putting air quotes around the word call.

"I will, sweetie." Alex says walking the short distance to his car. I wave good-bye and I can see Chris in the front seat, wrapping his arms around himself making a kissy face and Alex smacked him to quit. I walked over to a bench sitting down going through photos on my phone waiting for my cab.

Epilogue

By the time I land in Vegas, I have numerous text messages from Alex trying to set up our official first date. A smile comes to my face that he wants to go on a date. Alex mentions he is a nervous wreck to meet Xavier so early in our relationship. He knows how nervous I am about Xavier getting hurt so I am nervous about him meeting Xavier already too. I still think Halloween will be the best time for them to meet.

I walk out of the airport, my eyes browsing the lined-up cars trying to recognize my mom's car. I finally spot her car when I see her pull up to the curb in front of me, she must have just arrived. I step up to the car, pulling the trunk open to toss in my luggage before climbing into the passenger seat. I look in the back seat to see that Xavier is zonked out in his booster seat. I look back at my mom who pulls away from the curb to head home.

"Mom, I have a date on Tuesday. Could you watch Xavier?" I ask blatantly, breaking the silence in the car.

"Um, I'm sure that I can." She says with a smile, "Going on a date with a guy from the boat?"

"Yes." I answer.

"Consider it taken care of. Whenever you need babysitting for dates, I'll be there. Don't you worry." My mom says happily.

My mom pulls into the driveway of my house, I climb out to get my luggage as my mom wakes Xavier for me. Xavier gets out of the car, he sees me, and he's overcome with excitement. I kneel down waiting for him to run into my arms for a big hug. He runs into my arms hugging me tightly. I pick him up, carry him into the house with one arm, and pull my bag with the other.

Xavier follows me into my room and climbs onto my bed. Xavier tells me everything I've missed at school and daycare while I was gone.

I pull out the Lego Batmobile set Alex bought for Xavier.

"Is that mine?!"

"Yes, but we need to talk." I say as I stand in front of him.

"About what?"

"You know how you were asking me about dads before I went on the cruise?" I bite at my bottom lip trying to find a way to explain this to Xavier.

"Yes." He looks up at me with a confused expression.

"I met a boy that I really like. He knows about you, and he bought this for you."

"What's his name?"

"Alex."

"What does he do? Does he fix people like you?"

"No, he wrestles."

"What's that?" Xavier asks, I should have expected fifty questions.

"I'll show you." I say. I guess I should be fortunate that Alex

227

is famous because I can show Xavier who Alex is without them officially meeting. I pick my laptop up off my dresser, leading Xavier out to the living room to turn on some wrestling. I figure I can finish unpacking later. I want to spend quality time with my little man right now.

I connect my laptop to the SmartTV. I turn the laptop on and click the television on. I load up Pure Gold's website, navigate through it to find Alex's profile and click on one of his matches against Jim.

"Alex is the one with black hair." I say pointing to my boyfriend, at least I think he's my boyfriend. I sit down on my black leather couch, pulling my feet up onto the couch beside me. I am trying to watch the match as well, but Xavier's head is blocking some of the television from where I sit. I can hear Xavier talking to the television, I think he has found a new sport that he likes. My mom walks into the room with a book in hand.

"What's this?" My mom asks as she stops behind the love seat and takes notice of what is being played on the television.

"One of Alex's wrestling matches."

"Which one is he?"

"The one with black hair." I explain as my mom looks back at the television. I pull my phone out of my pocket, open the camera app, and take a picture of Xavier watching Alex wrestle.

Attaching the image to a text message, "'Xavier already adores you.'" I am hoping that seeing the picture will give Alex a bit of relief that Xavier is already rooting for him and will love him when they do meet.

Alex and I consistently text and talk on the phone. He shows up at my work to have lunch with me or to bring me food.

We have become even more serious after the cruise it seems. I think once we got off the boat, reality hit. The cruise was fun, but on land this is real life. Alex has proved to me time and time again that he has feelings for me by continuing to see me and blowing my phone up. Alex has even taken me out on a few dates, true one of the dates was going to watch him wrestle at Pure Gold.

My mother has been nothing but happy that I am going out. She is the number one fan for this relationship. Xavier is happy because he wants a dad more than anything. Plus, Alex being famous makes Xavier more ecstatic because he is going to have a famous person as a dad. Xavier watches Pure Gold every week to see Alex.

Today is Halloween and the first time that Alex will meet Xavier. Alex has been nothing but blowing my phone up with numerous texts expressing his nervousness about meeting Xavier. It is oddly cute that he is nervous to meet my son.

My mom volunteers to stay home to pass out candy while Alex and I take Xavier trick or treating. She is helping Xavier put on the Batman costume so I can get dressed. I pull on the white crop top shirt and the blue boy shorts. I reach for my makeup, applying what I know to make me look more realistically like Harley Quinn.

I brush my hair up into two pigtails. I grab the bat that I keep at my bedside walking out to grab a pillowcase to collect candy in. The doorbell sounds through the house; it is too early for kids to show up.

I head to the front door, pull the door open and standing on my porch is Alex. He actually showed up. Not only did he show up, but he is in costume. Alex has on black jeans with the metal chain dangling from the belt loop. A purple leather trench coat that goes to his knee. He has his hair gelled back, gold chain around his neck and no shirt exposing his upper body. He even put on makeup that resemble the pale skin and tattoos that the Jarod Leto Joker looks like.

"There's my Harley." He says with a smile. When he smiles, it exposes the gold grill he even popped in. I hunch over in laughter at the sight. He did it! He actually did it! He actually dressed up as the Joker for me. "What?"

"I need a picture." I say, grabbing my phone to get a picture of Alex.

"Mom?" Xavier asks. I turn around to see Xavier walking around the corner. He is in his full Batman costume. He steps up onto the foyer with me, I rest my hand on his shoulder as he steps beside me. I look up at Alex, his body tenses up a little from nerves. He truly is nervous to meet Xavier.

"Xavier, this is Alex." I say softly.

"No mom, that's the Joker." He says so matter of fact. All of us laugh.

"I know it's the Joker. Alex dressed up as the Joker to go trick or treating with us."

"I love that!" Xavier exclaims, jumping onto the front porch with Alex. Xavier grabs Alex's hand and gives it a tug. Alex takes the hint and kneels down in front of him, "I like you Alex, I'm happy you are coming with us." Xavier says, my heart melts.

"I'm happy I am coming too. Are you ready to go get some candy, bud?"

"Duh! Come on!" Xavier says, grabbing Alex's hand and tugging him towards the sidewalk to start trick or treating. Alex looks over his shoulder at me with a smile then turns back to Xavier who is chatting him up.

I feel my mom rest her hand on my shoulder, "He's going to be great with Xavier. I have never seen another man willingly dress up on Halloween for a girl. I don't even think that Dave dude would have done that."

"Leave it to Alex." I say with a chuckle.

"Joker and Batman are waiting on you." My mom says nudging me out the door. I jog to catch up to my party. I hold Xavier's other hand as we walk through the neighborhood hitting every house that has their light on.

"It's getting late, and you have school tomorrow." I say generally.

"I'm not tired though." Xavier whines, he is probably amped up from having so much fun and wanting to have Alex's ear. Xavier is really liking Alex and being the first time they met, Xavier probably has so much to say or ask Alex about everything.

"I'm getting very tired." Alex says, pretending to yawn.

"Me too." I say stretching out my arms.

Xavier huffs and rolls his eyes. "Fine."

We walk back through the neighborhood to my house. We walk up the walkway to the front door. Xavier lets himself in and I stand on the porch with Alex.

"You want to come in?" I ask hopefully. Alex smiles, but the smile creeps me out because of the fake gold teeth. He doesn't have to answer, his smile answers it for me. Alex steps into the house behind me. I can hear the water running from the guest bathroom, which means Xavier is taking his bath. "Now to inspect this candy."

I lead Alex into the kitchen, he leans back against the island to watch me inspect the candy. I reach for the big serving bowl, bring the bowl to the island to stand beside Alex. I pour the contents of the pillowcase into the bowl.

"I can go for a piece." Alex says as he grabs a piece out of the bowl not even caring what kind of candy it is. I roll my eyes as I begin to mix the candy up to give it a look over. I find something that catches my eye. I pull out a very expensive looking ring from the bowl, I just stare at it. This ring is definitely not the cheap twenty-five cent vending machine ring.

"Whoa, someone lost their ring in our bag. Who on my block is married?" I ask, beginning to rack my brain of all my neighbors.

"Actually," Alex begins to say. I look at Alex out of the corner of my eye. I see him push himself off the island and slide down to one knee.

"Stand up." I demand, he shakes his head no. I turn my body to face him, my body trembling in nerves and disbelief that this is happening.

"That's your ring if you say yes." He says staring up at me, his brown eyes the only thing I recognize of his due to all the makeup he has applied. "Girl, I'm a wrestler so I have bad knees."

"I thought that was only Chris." I joke, getting us to both laugh.

"Touché." He says with a couple more laughs.

"I thought I heard Alex out here." My mom says, startling me. Alex slides back to his feet, startling my mom. Her hand flings to cover her heart, "What were you doing?"

"I was asking your daughter for her hand in marriage." Alex answers truthfully, "But she hasn't answered yet."

"Mommy!! Is Alex staying the night? I want him to see the Batmobile he bought." Xavier exclaims, running into the room.

"Yes." I say generally.

"To him or to me?" Alex asks curiously.

"Both." I say happily. Alex grabs the ring off the counter to slide it onto my ring finger. After the ring was placed on my finger, I pulled Alex in for a rough passionate kiss. A smile spread across my lips after the kiss broke.

Alex stepped in front of Xavier and kneel down in front of him, "Xavier, may I be your dad?"

"Yes! You are on television and you like Batman. You'll be the best dad!"

"Well, I'm going to be your dad." Alex says, stretching out his arms. Xavier runs into them excitedly. Alex wraps Xavier in a big hug before picking Xavier up with him, "Now that Batmobile."

Made in the USA
Middletown, DE
08 April 2024